From The Streets Of Chambers Lane

From The Streets Of Chambers Lane

Daniel Maldonado

Copyright (C) 2017 Daniel Maldonado
Layout design and Copyright (C) 2021 by Next Chapter
Published 2021 by Next Chapter
Cover art by Cover Mint
Mass Market Paperback Edition
This book is a work of fiction. Names, characters, places, and incidents are the product of the author's imagination or are used fictitiously. Any resemblance to actual events, locales, or persons, living or dead, is purely coincidental.
All rights reserved. No part of this book may be reproduced or transmitted in any form or by any means, electronic or mechanical, including photocopying, recording, or by any information storage and retrieval system, without the author's permission.

This book is dedicated to my family and friends who struggled with me through a difficult time of my life. Thanks for listening, for being encouraging and for just being you.

Support Team

I would also like to thank the members of the Phoenix Valley Authors for all of the support, encouragement, ideas and critical reviews:

- Janine R. Pestel
- Bob Wilson
- Alicia Wright
- Karen Webster Longstreth
- Linda Curry

Contents

Chapter One: Jose Luis   1

Chapter Two: Lucia Maria   23

Chapter Three: Daniel   43

Chapter Four: Maria   63

Chapter Five: Randy   82

Chapter Six: Eduardo   99

Chapter Seven: Marie   118

Chapter Eight: Michael   136

Chapter Nine: Sachiko   145

Chapter Ten: Sylvia   158

Chapter Eleven: The Funeral   175

Chapter One

Jose Luis

When Jose Luis woke up, the putrid stench of the room filled his nostrils. He had lived in this squalid room at the local Motor Inn and Lodge for the past six months because the weekly rentals were cheap, and the motel manager did not mind if Jose Luis missed a week or two at times. There were not many renters and business was slow. If Jose Luis paid any missed week's rent in another week or secretly passed the manager a little bit of that doja they were both very fond of, Jose Luis was allowed to stay. Although the motel advertised room cleaning services on a weekly basis, the maids rarely came to clean the rooms or tidy up the motel. Jose Luis did not mind. He was used to the stench. He could no longer discern the commingled smell from the dark aqua green carpet (that hadn't been replaced in over a decade and which was repeatedly soiled from the dirt and debris endlessly tracked in from outside) with the aroma from the unsanitary water closet. The water closet's rusting and slightly broken porcelain throne betrayed its purported grandeur. The air was dank and unrecycled. The motel room stunk of body odor because all of the windows were tightly nailed shut and never opened, even though that was in violation of municipal ordinances.

Candy wrappers, soda cans, and other sundries were strewn all over the floor or tucked underneath the dark purple and orange floral comforter that covered the lumpy, full-sized mattress that was barely big enough for any traveler taller than an average height. A slight humming from the brown, Absocold compact refrigerator with its fake wood-look grain filled the confines of the diminutive room. A generic faux painting of the Appalachian landscape was askew over the bed at the far-left corner. Multiple dark, placid holes in the stucco betrayed where other picture frames previously hung but were stolen by past patrons. The long, vanilla drapes prevented what little sun that was out from entering the room. The burnt sienna door, which gave Jose Luis a false sense of security, was double-bolted.

As Jose Luis sat up on the edge of the mattress to pull on his faded skinny jeans, he noticed the blinking red light from the hospitality telephone that indicated he had missed a call and a voicemail message awaited. He pondered who had called and why he had not heard the phone ring. But then he remembered that the last night's festivities not only clouded his mind and memory, but also left a lingering and pervading smell of marijuana on his undergarments. He could barely smell it, but that was because the smell was too familiar to him and faded into his memory. Though he stayed up late that night watching several movies, the call must have come really early in the morning after he was deep in sleep and he was no longer cognizant of his surroundings; the escape he so longed for. He struggled to put on the tight, black shirt that no longer fit him. He still wore the shirt because he had no money to buy newer clothes. He was too proud to visit the local YMCA for free used, donated clothes. He also put on his light blue plaid jacket with the hoodie that he never wore unless it rained. He then pulled the handset to his ear, pushed the necessary buttons to get the message, and listened attentively.

"Hey Junior. It's me, Daniel. Sorry to call you so early. Something has come up. I really need to talk to you. Call me."

The voice was recognizable, but Jose Luis rarely heard it these past three years. He and his younger brother stopped speaking because Jose Luis was mad at Daniel for siding with Maria, their older sister. Daniel agreed that Jose Luis should move out of Maria's house and get his own place. How dare he take Maria's side?!! Didn't Daniel know how hard Jose Luis was trying to find a second job and how much money he was working as a commissioned sales associate at Sears in their appliance department? Jose Luis occasionally sold mattresses at a higher commission. He was very proud of the extra money that he earned. It didn't matter that Jose Luis only was slotted to work ten hours a week for the past few months. If he could earn a full week's pay in commissions as he oftentimes claimed, why should he have to work forty hours like those seemingly foolish employees who were not as good or successful as he was? Jose Luis thought of himself as a hard worker and would let anyone know it if they were willing to listen to him speak about it endlessly. Jose Luis believed that he could sell anyone anything, especially elderly couples who blindly trusted him with his fast and slick purported understanding of their needs. According to Jose Luis, money was pouring in hand over fist even if no one in the family believed him. But that certainly was not a reason why he had to move out and be on his own and pay for everything himself. At least that was what Jose Luis truly believed. He was perfectly content with living with Maria and her husband even though she was not.

Jose Luis Mendoza was a tall, strapping Puerto Rican male in his mid-forties. He towered over the other members of the family at six foot one. No one knew why he was so much taller than the other kids in the family. Some relatives suspected that it was because he had a different father. He also did not have the button nose that his mom, Maria, and Daniel all had. Jose Luis had a hawk nose that appeared to look pointed when viewed from the side. It made him look different from the rest of the family. However, Jose Luis apparently looked identical to his namesake, which is why everyone called him Junior.

The thought that he was not related was often dismissed, but occasionally resurfaced sometimes over the years. Because he had given the only family picture of his father to his first girlfriend, Gladys, no one could actually confirm that Jose Luis looked like his father. That did not matter to him.

The handsomeness of his youth had dimly faded, but in Jose Luis's mind, he was as handsome as ever and every woman knew it. But he had gained significant weight over the years. His slick, black hair was styled in a mini ponytail that hung just passed his neck and that was tied with a crusty, red rubber band that he refused to replace. He no longer sported the sparse goatee that he wore in his early thirties. He still had his thin mustache that was really a collection of peach-fuzz hair, which he often contemplated darkening with mascara to give himself an older and wiser look. Even when he was indoors, he would wear dark shades perhaps to conceal his never ceasing bloodshot eyes. He simply claimed that it was to make himself look younger and that no one could really handle the suave, but unsophisticated attitude that he exuded.

In his younger days, Jose Luis had an 80's sweat-locker look with a black leather glove that he wore on his right hand as if he was trying to emulate Michael Jackson. At times his wardrobe reflected the star of his favorite cult-classic movie, Purple Rain. Jose Luis wore the same flowing big hair but without the white, ruffled shirt or Apollonia at his side. He even still wore mascara on his eyelashes and faint eye makeup because one could see the smudges underneath his eyes when he woke up this morning. Jose Luis had poor dental hygiene and rarely brushed his teeth or flossed resulting in dimly yellowed teeth that he thought no one noticed. Smoking pot did not help with the discoloration.

No one believed a word he said because his comments were belied by the persistent pungent yet skunky smell of marijuana that pervaded his body with its indistinguishable crisp and sharp undertone that some mistake as the smell of an elderly person's home. It was often worsened by his refusal to regularly shower or change his clothes and his increased perspiration. He often layered his clothes even during hot summer days. Jose Luis thought that he could mask the putrid smell by religiously spraying his outerwear with cheap, water-downed cologne and using Listerine breaths strips as if they were candy. But it was of no avail.

When he had finished dressing, Jose Luis pondered whether he should call his younger brother back. Though they were separated by less than a year in age, their personality differences were such that people did not believe that they were brothers or even related. Even Jose Luis felt that estrangement. The recent years of separation made it worse. Because Jose Luis was the cause of that separation, his resolved waned. But just then a slight rapping at the door disturbed his thoughts. He looked towards the door worried that it may have been someone asking him to repay them money. Jose Luis would often borrow from his friends under false pretenses. He would also swindle money from his family with glee. Despair would overcome him once his family and friends learned of his thievery. Jose Luis would then feign outrage to desperately divert from his scoundrous ways.

Who could it be at the door and what did they want? He pondered not opening the door and pretending that the room was empty. Had it been the often unseen maid service, she would have opened the door by now with her own master key. So it was clearly not the maid. That thought made Jose Luis even more anxious and suspicious. Then he heard another rapping and tried to stealthily walk towards the door to see who it was. He dared not open the drapes for fear of being revealed. The door lacked a peephole. Perhaps if he drew near, then he could hear any rumblings outside and discern the mysterious visitor's intention.

"Open the door. I know you are in there. I can hear you moving around. Don't think you are being slick about it!"

"What do you want?"

"Didn't you get my voicemail message?"

"Yeah, but you never said that you were coming over."

"It's important and I was worried that something was up once you never called me back."

Jose Luis unbolted one lock and then the other and opened the door. Now askew, the opened door let some of the fresh air into the room and released some stale odors along with it. Daniel knew that familiar, reeking smell. He despised it and the expected forthcoming shenanigans. But the day's events were required, and his purpose predestined.

"I see that you are already dressed. That's good."

"Like I need your approval."

Daniel did not wait to be invited in. He pushed the door wider, walked deeper into the room, and paced a little, while trying to avoid the trash and clothes strewed on the floor. Daniel's eyes quickly gazed around the motel room with hopes of discerning his brother's state of mind. Daniel also wanted to gather information about anything that could be used against Jose Luis if the situation required it.

"Sit down."

"Where?"

"Anywhere. You must be exhausted from the drive."

Daniel pushed some filthy clothes off of a chair and looked down before sitting.

"Want anything to drink? I don't have anything but soda." Jose Luis opened the small fridge, took out two cans of Diet Coke, handed one to his brother, and then gulped down the other one.

Daniel watched this whole ceremony wondering what would be next and what horror story would come forth as yet another excuse that Daniel would have to endure and then recall years later as evidence of Jose Luis's persistent denial and lies easily unwoven and unraveled.

"I see that you are still stealing spoils from your job." Daniel was referring to the Coke cans.

For seven years, Jose Luis had worked for Coca Cola as a driver delivering merchandise to the various stores and restocking the shelves. He loved the job because it gave him unfettered access to each store with little to no oversight from his employer or the store's local management. Jose Luis could walk in unnoticed and unsuspected, inspect the floor for missing product, unload what that store needed for the week, and then go on his merry way. If it took him three hours to complete his route, Jose Luis would bill eight hours. No one was the wiser. Who could know where he was or what he was doing? Most of the time he was actually just playing video games in his room when he claimed that he was working.

But this time, things were different. In some ways, Jose Luis was excited that his brother was here and that he could explain it all if Daniel would just listen and be supportive.

"I can no longer work there."

"*Not again,*" Daniel muttered to himself. "Did you quit?"

"No. They fired me. That's what I want to talk to you about. You're a lawyer. Don't you know any lawyers here in California?"

"I only know a few, but I can ask someone to recommend one if you really need one."

"I do. I think I have a great case. So great that you should take it." Jose Luis grinned in excitement.

"I'm pretty selective of the cases that I take. Besides, I'm not licensed to practice in California. Only in Arizona." Daniel did not bother to say that he was also licensed in Nevada. It did not really matter in the end. He already knew that, whatever his brother was going to say, Daniel did not want to get involved in it. "*Yes, a referral is all that I'm going to do. He is family. At least he won't be able to say I never helped him,*" Daniel thought to himself with a slight sense of pride.

"After you hear this, I'm sure that you will want to take it. We're going to make a lot of money. We'll be rich." Daniel doubted that but did not say so because he wanted to appear objective. He also did not want to prejudge the situation even though he was skeptical.

"Tell me what happened."

"Well, I went into Von's at Figueroa and Central to restock the Coke products. One of the managers stopped me and told me that this female employee complained that I cursed her out. I told him that I didn't. But he insisted. She was lying and he believed her over me. So I was fired for that."

"Why? Doesn't your manager like you?"

"Well, he isn't my manager. He is the store manager at Von's. He works for Von's, not for Coke."

"If he works for Von's, then he can't fire you."

"He didn't fire me. He called Coke and complained and then I was fired."

"What did you tell your manager at Coke?"

"I told him that she was lying, that she always lies and wants to get me in trouble."

"Why would she do that?"

"I think she likes me."

"So she likes you and tried to get you fired? That doesn't make sense."

"I don't like her. She's fat and has kids. And I don't want that. So she is making this up to get back at me."

"Didn't you tell the Von's manager that?"

"He won't believe me because I am black."

"You're not black, Junior. You're Hispanic." Daniel's stern look betrayed his subtle anger.

"He doesn't care. I'm black to him and he doesn't like black people."

"So he's white, I take it? Did you tell your manager that?"

"I didn't have to. He knows the guy is racist."

"Why do you say that?"

"It's obvious. He always says bad things about how black people are no good, steal, are lazy, and are on welfare. He was looking for a way to get me out of that store and this was his chance."

"So why didn't they just give that store to another driver so that you didn't have to deal with the manager? I thought you said that you are a good worker and Coke needs you and won't get rid of you because no one works as hard as you. They didn't need to fire you for a mistake especially because you deny saying it. What did she claim you said to her?"

"She said I called her a bitch."

"Well, did you?"

"I did. But that's because she was acting like one and being mean to me. She wanted me to make sure that the Coke products were fully stocked and I told her that I stocked them earlier in the week and that I couldn't come back until next week. She felt like I wasn't concerned about their customers and that I was being lazy."

"So why couldn't you do that store twice that week?"

"I didn't feel like it. Why should I? It's not like they are going to pay me twice to go there?" Jose Luis was adamant and proud of it.

"So what did your manager say when you told him that you didn't want to do the store twice and that you did curse at the female employee?"

"I told him that I was tired of listening to a manager who couldn't stand up to people and allowed his favorites to get away with things while hard workers like myself have to do all of the work." Jose Luis stood up and anxiously paced around the motel room. "I am a hard worker," he insisted. "No one knows the job like me. And he put me on days when I told him that I only wanted to work nights because I am going to culinary school during the day and need to work at night. There are plenty of guys who can work the day shift and who want to work days, but he put me on days. And then he had the nerve to cut my hours. So I told him that I am going to work the hours he gives me, but bill the company whatever I want to bill and there is nothing that he can do about it."

"You told your boss that?!!"

"Yeah. He had nothing to say." Jose Luis said this as if he was very proud of himself for confronting his boss.

"And you think you are going to sue your company for wrongful termination and discrimination and win? You don't have a case."

"What do you mean I don't have a case? They fired me because they think I am black. They are racist."

"Junior, you called that woman a bitch."

"Yeah."

"You basically told your boss that you were going to steal from the company. What do you think he was going to do? Fire you. That's what I would tell your company to do if I was their attorney and they asked me what to do."

"You're not going to take my case?"

"No. Why would I?"

"You're my brother."

"I only take cases that have merit. I can't go in front of a jury asking them to rule in your favor when you cursed out that woman and threatened to steal your company's money by cheating them. No jury would believe you were fired because of racism."

"What about referring me to another attorney?"

"No way. I would be a laughing stock. No attorney would ever take any other case that I would refer to them if they learned that I knew the truth."

"What the hell are you good for then? I've been there for you your entire life and you've never been here for me. Not you. Not mom. Not Maria. When are you guys going to be here for me?"

Daniel resisted the strong urge to curse Jose Luis out. He was used to these incessant tirades when Jose Luis would not get his way. First, there was the modeling career when Jose Luis claimed that he worked out, got a six pack, and modeled swim wear for a catalog that never came out. Jose Luis never revealed the name of the company that he purportedly modeled for. So no one in the family could confirm this non-existent modeling career. He fancied himself like Tyson Bedford or sometimes Marcus Schenkenberg. But there were no photos. No catalogs. No go sees. Just the worthless words that Jose Luis kept spouting and the praise that he wanted everyone to lavish upon him undeservedly. When Daniel confronted Jose Luis after he claimed the catalog was out, Jose Luis could not give an answer. He could not produce the catalog. He instead lashed out at Daniel with every curse word that Jose Luis knew. Some of the curse words were in Spanish.

Then there was that culinary school where Jose Luis never really applied to. He never actually attended, but he insisted to everyone in the family that he had been attending culinary school. Jose Luis could never seem to produce the letter of acceptance or any report card or proof that he paid any tuition. And then there was the hot dog stand that Jose Luis wanted to buy. He claimed that he was a good cook and that everyone loved his cooking. Daniel had never seen Jose Luis cook once nor tasted any food that he ever cooked. Or the time when he worked for Home Depot and claimed that after three months he was going to be promoted to department manager because he was such a good worker. He was fired a week later for refusing to heed his manager's wishes. Or the time when he joined the Army and went to boot camp. He quickly chose to be honorably discharged because the wool exacerbated his eczema and caused him to itch all over his body. Never mind that he longed for his under-aged girlfriend at home on Chambers Lane. He chose instead to leave the military because he wanted to be with her. The military doctors could have treated Jose Luis's eczema and stabilized his condition. He regretted that decision years later.

Jose Luis was a quitter. Most of his jobs lasted only three months. But for some reason, he worked at Coke for nearly seven years. It was the longest job that he ever had. Everyone was surprised that he lasted even that long. Perhaps it was because one of Jose Luis's co-worker was a drug dealer and sold Jose Luis marijuana in exchange for routes. Perhaps it was because the job gave him the freedom that he longed for which he did not have at a regular nine-to-five job. Or perhaps it was because he was actually good at the job. Jose Luis could have made it a long standing career if it wasn't for his oversized ego that did not match his character.

"Look at me. I'm living in this rat hole. No one comes to visit me. This is the first time you have even bothered to visit me in years."

"Junior, you didn't listen to me when I told you to get a full time job and to settle down with that girl from your church. What was her name? Yolanda? Yes, you liked her and her three kids. She liked you a lot and wanted to marry you. Why didn't you marry her like you said you would?"

"She was a hypocrite. She would text guys all the time flirting with them, claim that she was just friends. But if I texted a woman, she would get jealous and angry and claimed I was having sex with the woman. She was the one who was cheating. Maybe not sexually, but at least emotionally. She would keep promising to stop texting those guys, but I would see her texting them and then she would get mad at me if I told her about it. She would first deny it and promise me again that she wouldn't text them. Then she would say that I was trying to control her and prevent her from having any male friends. She would always bring up how her ex cheated on her with another woman from church and how she didn't feel beautiful or loved…"

Jose Luis could talk for hours repeating the same story over and over again. Asking the same questions *ad nauseum*. Did she like me? Should I be with her? Does she love me? I love her kids, but will they respect me as a dad when I am not their dad? Did she like me? Over and over until the sun would set. The only thing that saved the telephone conversation would be the dying battery that needed to be recharged.

"I didn't come here to talk about your job or Yolanda," Daniel interrupted.

"Then why are you here?" Jose Luis was upset that he was interrupted but was anxious to know why Daniel traveled the long distance to his motel.

"I wanted to let you know that Maria called me. She spoke to mom and, unfortunately, Michael is dead." Silence filled the room.

Jose Luis sat down at the edge of the frumpy bed and gazed at the floor. "Why are you telling me?"

"He is our brother. What do you mean 'why am I telling you?' Have some sympathy and respect."

Jose Luis knew that Michael was their youngest brother. Daniel's revelation was not anything new. Jose Luis simply lacked the compassion for others other than himself.

"What do you want me to do about that? I have no money." Jose Luis looked around the motel room with his arm outstretched as if to point out the obvious destitution which confirmed this fact.

"I'm not asking you for money." Daniel knew that even if Jose Luis had some money that he would never offer it even in this time of need. "Mom wants to know if you are going to the funeral."

"I can't afford to fly to Atlanta."

"Mom's church is having a memorial in Atlanta, but Michael is going to be buried here."

"I'm not sure if I am going to go."

"Why not?"

"You know why."

Jose Luis was probably ashamed to relay the story again. Or perhaps he was tired of saying this nearly half-decade-old story that he held quick to the heart.

Daniel thought it was silly and asinine. Years ago, Jose Luis also lived in Atlanta with his mom and youngest brother, Michael. But Jose Luis felt ostracized because he lived in the basement. Michael and their mother lived upstairs in the three bedroom home that she rented. The basement room where Jose Luis lived was spacious and bigger than the master suite. It even had its own entrance and direct access to the backyard. Jose Luis believed that he was relegated to the basement. He resented it because of the flooring was cold and damp. The flooring was really just painted cement with no carpeting or tile. In some ways, Jose Luis thought of himself like a cinderfella or even the black sheep of the family. He viewed the basement room as being hidden away even though guests rarely came to the house. To add insult to injury, Jose Luis felt that the $200 a month rent that he paid to his mother was excessive. Why couldn't he live there for free even if he was a grown man? Michael didn't have to pay rent. So why should he? Paying rent, Jose Luis thought, entitled him to do whatever he wanted in the house. He wanted to smokie weed, which his mother forbade adamantly. Jose Luis also felt that everyone, including Michael, should listen to him and do what he said even though Michael was a teenager at the time.

Jose Luis was not the ideal, oldest brother. He lost jobs all the time, argued over minuscule things, had uncontrollably rage, but most of all was manipulative to no end. Jose Luis often took advantage of Michael. He knew that Michael had not seen his father in years and that Michael desperately wanted a father figure. Although Jose Luis was not Michael's father, Jose Luis was twenty-four years his senior. Michael wanted to look up to Jose Luis even if it meant taking up that nasty smoking habit at the young age of fourteen. Jose Luis would promise to take Michael to the movies or to dinner. He gave every excuse in the book to avoid taking Michael anywhere because he was cheap. Jose Luis ended up wasting the little money that he had on lavish gifts to his female friends. These women had no interest in him other than getting some of his paltry money. If Michael was older and had a job, Jose Luis would have used those opportunities to swindle Michael out of his money and trick Michael to pay for the movies or a good meal. Without that option, Jose Luis's only tactic to avoid his promises was simply to make himself scarce and to say, "Next week" when Michael finally caught up to him. After a while, Michael realized what Jose Luis was doing, but still longed to spend time with his oldest brother.

Jose Luis only had time to spend with Michael when he needed an opponent to play against in a video game or if Jose Luis did not want to watch a DVD movie by himself. Of course, none of the activities cost Jose Luis any money. That fact did not escape Michael. But when Jose Luis started working nights and on the weekends, he had even less time to spend with Michael. One Friday night while Jose Luis was working, Michael walked down to the basement, entered Jose Luis's room, and took several DVDs.

That night, Michael watched the movies in his own room on his TV with his own DVD player. He enjoyed the alone time that the house gave to him that evening, sipped soda, and ate buttered popcorn. After the solemnity of that long evening that ended in the early hours the next morning, Michael fell asleep; forgetting to return the DVDs. Weeks later, Jose Luis finally noticed that some of his DVDs were missing. He looked everywhere for them until he finally found them in Michael's room. Enraged by what he perceived as a betrayal beyond measure, in revenge, Jose Luis urinated in the DVD player; ruining it so that it was no longer usable.

"Take that," he said to himself gleefully, hoping it would teach Michael a lesson. "How dare he steal from me?"

Daniel heard the story many times. He anticipated that Jose Luis would repeat this story as his excuse why he would not attend the funeral. Daniel exclaimed, "He didn't steal your DVDs. He just borrowed them. You could still use them. It's not like he broke them or sold them. I can't believe that you did that. That was disgusting and immature of you. You're a grown man and Michael was a kid. You were supposed to be a positive role model for him. I don't even know why mom even let you stay with her. You didn't even buy the DVDs anyway. I gave them all to you for free after you begged me for them. So if anyone should be mad, I should be."

Tired of this scolding over the years, Jose Luis sighed in desperation. "I know. I know. But they were my DVDs and he had no right to take them. He needed to learn a lesson."

"I can't believe that you never apologized. Does mom know that you did that?"

"She's your mother." Jose Luis never answered, not that day or any other previous day when he first told Daniel and Daniel inquired of him. Daniel was too embarrassed to bring up the subject to his mother. Years later, after Jose Luis moved back to Georgia from California on yet another whim, their mother did tell Daniel that she knew what Jose Luis had done to Michael's DVD player. But in the interim, Daniel never knew if she was aware of Jose Luis's shenanigans.

"Fine. Come to the funeral if you want. Don't come if you don't want to. Just don't wear that purple suit that you wore to Maria's wedding. It's inappropriate." Daniel wanted to also let Jose Luis know not to wear the accompanying single, white glove that he also wore to the wedding. But Daniel did not want to press the issue.

"What are you talking about? That's a great suit," Jose Luis added.

"Maria doesn't want you coming in your purple suit."

"Maria doesn't control me. She thinks she is my mom and says that she took care of us when we were kids. She didn't cook for us; she didn't help us with our homework; she didn't encourage us to do well in our lives, or in any way act like a mother to us. So I don't know why she keeps saying she was a mom to us after all these years. I don't consider her my mother. I'm going to do what I want, not what Maria wants. I moved here to this motel because I don't want to listen to her anymore. I love my sister, but I love myself more."

Daniel could not disagree with Jose Luis. So he walked out of the motel room onto the dusty road to his car and drove home.

Chapter Two

Lucia Maria

Gone was the ornate alter with its multiple statues of Jesus and the Virgin Mary along with the other myriad of unknown saints who were the patron saints of someone or something of the other. There were no longer the candles lit in a row on tall, golden candle holders reminiscent of chalices once utilized during the Roman Empire. The colorful, ceramic seraphim adorned with human faces prostrating both their wings in a similar attempt to cover the alter were also not there. Nor was there any humongous wooden cross with the letters "INRI" emblazoned upon it. Or the intricate stained glass windows consisting of mica, alabaster, shell, and other translucent materials nestled inside lead ferraments in order to depict various religious themes or historical events such as the Via Dolorosa or the Crusades. There were no pictures of the Last Supper or other significant moments of Jesus' life. The scent of lavender, cedar, frankincense, and myrrh wafting from brass censers hung from chains and swung by the priests ever so slightly to incense the alter was also gone. Because she had no longer attended a Catholic mass in over twenty years, Lucia Maria Sheffield no longer witnessed such things when she now attended church. In its place was a simple cross hanging on the wall behind a wooden lectern where her pastor, William Brown, would give his weekly sermons. Just behind the lectern, there were plain wooden chairs with beige, upholstered manchettes and seat cushions. There was also a long wooden table where the circular, aluminum stacking communion trays and bread plates would be placed on a monthly basis for one of the few sacraments that were observed. Her current church did not take communion ever week like her Catholic Church. So these times were more precious and solemn to her. Two rows of similarly upholstered beige chairs filled the northern most part of the chancel in the loft where the choir would sing in simple, antique white polyester choir robes with blue stoles. The church was very plain and not ornate like most traditional churches. However, every April the chancel would be adorned with trumpet-shaped Easter lilies. The pastor would remind the small congregation that these beautiful flowers grew in the Garden of Gethsemane where the Lord frequently prayed at night alone away from his disciples.

At this time of day on a Tuesday, there were no other people at the Pentecostal church where Lucia attended. She came here at this time to purposefully avoid any crowds or any of her friends. If anyone saw her, they would surely wonder why Lucia was there because it was uncharacteristic of her to be at church during the week. Lucia would normally be at one of the many bible studies that she attended at various members' homes. But today, she sat on the last pew in the rear of the church. Her normal spot on Sundays was in the third row. In the third row, she could hear Pastor Brown better and ruminate on his sermons while taking notes. But the rear pew gave Lucia a view of the entire sanctuary. The view helped her focus on her thoughts rather than her emotions. She had been feeling overwhelmed these past few days since Michael's death. Alone, at her church, gave her some sense of comfort and reassurance that was absent when she was at work or at home. Doubts of why and whether she could endure it entered her mind. These thoughts were like a cyclone destroying everything in its wake including the stoic faith she had all of these decades. She began to ponder her life and the choices that she made. She blamed herself for the outcome. Had she made better choices when she was younger, listened to God sooner or more often rather than her fleshly desires, or if she had not given in to the unceasing loneliness that she felt which clouded her judgment, perhaps this would have never come to pass. Would Michael had even been born in the first place if temptation's lure wasn't so inescapable? Maybe not. But her mind did not realize that the different choices that she could have made would have meant different outcomes altogether rather than just different circumstances.

Would she still have had all five of her children? Had she never been forced to marry at the young age of sixteen, then, of course, her first three children would not have been the same. They may have had a different father or may have never been born in the first place. Instead of focusing on that, she instead focused on what it would have meant to her experiences if she had not married Jose Luis Mendoza, Senior. She would not have endured the many beatings from him. He apparently learned this behavior from watching his own father beat his mother. He mimicked that behavior during his own marriage to Lucia when he succumbed to anger. She would have never moved back to New York from Los Angeles with him and the kids to find his long, lost mother who apparently wanted nothing to do with him. Lucia often regretted putting that ad in the newspaper hoping to locate his mother. If she had not placed that ad, then Jose Luis would have never found his mother and would have never wanted to move back to New York. He never would have listened to his mother's counsel and abandoned Lucia and the kids. Lucia would never get over that abandonment which she carried in every other relationship since.

Why would a mother counsel her nineteen year old son to leave his wife and three young kids when she never really knew them? Lucia could only imagine that it was because the mother wanted him all to herself. She had not seen her son since he was five years old. Perhaps the guilt of abandoning her son drew her, at that moment now that they were finally reunited, to smother him, rather than accept that he was now an adult with his own family. His longing to please his mother also clouded his judgment. So Jose Luis decided that he no longer wanted to be married and the very next morning told Lucia that. Lucia took the three kids in a cab and traveled to her brother's house in Brooklyn. She stayed there until she had enough money to travel cross country again. Once in California, she rented a converted garage in downtown Los Angeles. All four of them stayed in that small, dank room.

Lucia could honestly say that she never really loved Jose Luis. How could she? She never had the chance to fall in love with him before the beatings started. She never knew why he asked Lucia's mother for her hand in marriage. They were both sixteen. They meet each other once or twice while at high school and never really went on a date together before they were married. Lucia's mother was fed up raising her own kids. When she was in her midforties, Lucia's mother wanted to marry her children all off so that she could be single and unattached again and spend the time with her lover, Antonio. The oldest daughter, Isabel, ran off with her black boyfriend after she learned that she was pregnant. Her mother insisted that Isabel get an abortion and marry someone else other than an African-American. The middle daughter, Belén, was married off to a divorcee who supposedly had no children from his first marriage. Lucia thought she could escape this nonsense of getting married off because she was the youngest. At sixteen, Lucia still had aspirations of graduating from high school and attending college. She dreamt of having her own career, perhaps as a journalist or even a botanist. She longed for something that would take her away from her squalid life with her mother and the rest of her siblings. All of that came to an end with the knock at the door from Jose Luis that evening when he asked to marry her. Somehow he had found out that Lucia's mother was trying to get rid of her children. On his own, Jose Luis thought that marriage to Lucia would solve his own problems. Later that week, Lucia's mother gave her consent to the magistrate. The two were married at a simple civil wedding. It was nothing like the grand wedding in a Catholic church that Lucia had always dreamed of since she was a young child.

Had she never married Jose Luis, then she never would have had three children when she met Marcelo Robles, Sylvia's father. Marcelo was younger and was from South America. He could speak perfect English albeit with an accent that she thought was sexy. His curly hair, dark brown eyes, slender lips, and boisterous laughter wooed Lucia with little effort. He was introduced to Lucia by her older sister, Belén, who also worked at the same warehouse as Marcelo. It did not matter to Lucia that Marcelo worked the graveyard shift on Friday and Saturday nights. The money he earned at the warehouse allowed him to make up for the lonely nights. He would shower Lucia with gifts, take her and the kids out to the movies or to McArthur Park, and then for a bite to eat at an A&W restaurant. Sure, Marcelo had a baby blue MGB that only seated two. He drove the MG on occasion instead of his classic Chevy Bel Air with its long rear fins that appear to jet into the sunset. Even though the MG was impractical for Lucia and her three kids, the sports car that Marcelo drove on the weekends only added to his allure. She fell in love with him like when teenagers succumb to puppy love in high school for the first time, even though she was twenty-six years old at the time.

But after Lucia became pregnant with Sylvia, Marcelo changed. He decided that he did not want to marry a woman who already had three kids with all the accompanying issues that such a relationship entailed. He wanted to start his own family rather than inherit one. Although in later years when he was in his fifties, Marcelo claimed to have truly loved Lucia at the time. But he could not escape the thought of having his own family. He secretly began an affair with a single Hispanic woman at his job who had no kids. He would secretly meet with her on his days off, all the while telling Lucia that he was working. Once Sylvia was born, Marcelo would take Sylvia to spend some time alone with her. But in reality, Marcelo would spend the day with Sylvia and his girlfriend. Lucia learned of the affair after Daniel saw Marcelo driving in the MG with Sylia and his girlfriend when they drove passed Ramona Elementary School where Daniel attended. Lucia was devastated. She often wondered why Marcelo never proposed or never seemed too excited about having a baby with her. Their relationship drastically changed after Sylvia's birth. Marcelo seemed so distant. Their relationship never recovered. Marcelo married his girlfriend a few years later. However, she could actually never get pregnant. They ended up divorced and childless decades later.

These thoughts swirled around as Lucia bowed her head. She silently prayed to herself at the back of the church. A few tears streaked from her eyes. She used all of her inner fortitude to hold them back. She feared that she would ultimately allow herself to drown her sorrows in a plaintive wail that would arouse even greater concerns in such a public place. A part of her hoped someone would walk in and comfort her. She knew that the possibility was slim. She waited for someone. She thought maybe her pastor or someone from the church staff would walk by. But no one came. After awhile, she opened her purse and removed her small, worn bible that she brought everywhere with her. She thumbed through her bible until she reached the familiar book of Isaiah. She began reading to herself:

He will swallow up death for all time,
And the Lord GOD will wipe tears away from all faces,
And He will remove the reproach of His people from all the earth;
For the LORD has spoken.

She repeated the words to herself until they brightened her spirit. She began to long for the day when the truth of those verses were a reality; when her own tears would forever fade away. Michael, her youngest son, had promised that he would never leave her and that he would be with her always. Her other children had moved on with their lives, had gotten married, or had kids. For some reason, she held Michael to that child-like promise at this moment even though it was unrealistic.

"Why did you leave me, Michael?" she muttered; hoping he would somehow answer or perhaps the Lord himself would respond and clarify the reason.

An overwhelming sense of anxiety overtook her as she wondered what her life would be now without her youngest son. Wearied by the sleepless nights, Lucia continued. "Lord, you should have taken me. It's not right for a mother to outlive her children and bury them. I don't know what to do. Please give me strength and Your Wisdom."

The ache in her heart grew stronger. The only avenue of comfort that she could think of was to remember her youngest son. She remembered his strawberry blond, curly hair which he got from his Caucasian father. Michael's hair frizzed more often once they moved to Marietta, Georgia. She remembered when he was a child and how he loved to play with his Teddy Ruxpin, the animatronic teddy bear that he got as a Christmas gift from Daniel when he was two. She remembered the way that Michael would hopelessly try to fit in with the teenage boys his age and pretended to be fully white the way that his father was. However, every student and teacher could see that his mother was a Latina. Michael refused to learn to speak Spanish or even admit that he was Hispanic. Instead, while living in California, Michael only had white friends. When he was thirteen and in middle school, his group of friends fancied themselves as neo-Nazis. They painted swastikas on several local homes until the police arrested the whole lot of them. His mother was surprised to find out that Michael was ashamed about being part Hispanic. But his curly hair gave away that he was not 100% white. There was nothing he could do about it, but deny it vehemently.

After the swastika incident, Michael began a slow, downward spiral. There was the incident when he tried to set fire to the neighbor's house or when he abused another neighbor's tabby and swung it in circles by the tail. Then there was the time he stuffed firecrackers in the external door of the school cafeteria, lite them so that the door mysteriously opened, and then pretended with his other friends to be line cooks passing out invisible food for fun to invisible children, some of whom were his classmates. Luckily, they left before anyone found out or the cops came. Or the time when he broke into the local liquor store late one Thanksgiving evening when Lucia was away in Tijuana, Mexico for the weekend with one of her boyfriends. Michael came home with a large box of Snickers and no cash or anything of real value. The other siblings mocked Michael for such an unprofitable endeavor. The laughter ensued when Michael decided to throw the box of candy into the neighbor's yard for fear that the cops would find the evidence of his bungled robbery in his own home. He also became more aggressive after his growth spurt when he became freakishly taller than the rest of the kids in school, including his substantially older siblings. But his new found height only reminded him of his absent father who was just as tall and obese, but who also had a boyish face and an immature demeanor.

Michael despised his father. His father left Lucia when Michael was seven years old to be in an open relationship with a man. Lucia's family repeatedly suspected that he was gay, but she adamantly denied it, ignored any signs, and married him anyway. When Michael's dad left with his lover, Lucia could not believe it and went into shock. She lost tremendous amounts of weight from the anxious nights, wondering if he would come back to her and whether she should take him back. They had been married for seven years and got engaged shortly after she learned that she was pregnant. Lucia considered Michael a miracle baby because she had him at forty-three years old and thought she could not have any more children. Her eldest, Maria, was already twenty-five when Lucia got pregnant and Sylvia, the youngest, was sixteen.

Lucia met Michael's father when she lived in Canyon Country on Sierra Highway. The mobile home that she owned sat on nineteen acres which was mostly hilly and unusable. But she had a goat, chickens, rabbits, and other animals there and pretended to live a country life not too far from the city. She never harvested any of the animals and considered that cruel. She raised them only as pets and named them all. After years of living there alone, she met Michael's father when he came to her house to deliver propane gas for the winter months. She liked his boyish charm and his constant joking. When he lost the delivery job with the propane company, she let him move in. They married later that year after she became pregnant. She quit her job as a teacher's assistant to be a stay-at-home mom taking care of Michael.

The marital relationship splintered as they often do after the birth of a child. Michael's father got a job working at a dealership in North Hollywood. His daily commute was an hour one way. The job kept him away for long hours into the night especially on the weekends. Then there was the late night happy hours with his friends or coworkers. Michael's father would forget to call and say that he was coming home late. He would also conveniently forget to let Lucia know that he spent a little too much money so that the bills could not be paid. Lucia considered it her wifely duty to stay at home and take care of Michael like a good Christian woman. Without a job, she was wholly dependent on Michael's father to pay the bills. This was the first time in her adult life when she was not independent. She had prayed mightily that God would give her the strength to be patient and loving when Michael's father would not come home or when he would not pay the bills. It gave her anxiety nonetheless.

When he lost the job at the dealership, Michael's father could not find or more accurately would not find a job for nearly two years. He saw the break as a time to spend with Michael. He did not want to miss out on anymore of Michael's childhood like when he was working long hours at the dealership. Besides, he knew that Lucia had cashed out her retirement fund when she quit her job to raise Michael. But when one month of unemployment turned into three months and then four, Michael's father began spending even more nights at the bar, leaving Lucia and his son alone more often. Because they were unable to pay the mortgage after two years, Lucia lost her home that she bought before she met Michael's father. She was angered by his mismanagement of their money. They moved into a small, two-bedroom apartment in town and she had to give away all of the animals that she had come to love and sell some of their furniture. Less than thirty days later, Michael's father came clean and finally admitted to Lucia that he was gay and had a lover. She feared that he lost her home purposefully in order to sabotage the marriage and go his separate way and that angered her even more. Why couldn't he had just been honest with her from the beginning rather than force her to lose her house in order to move on with his life and pursue his gay lifestyle?

So when Sylvia called several months later saying that she was pregnant with her second child, Lucia took that opportunity to move cross country to Georgia and get away from the familiar surroundings and to be near her new grandchild. She had nothing to lose and wanted to start over in a new town where no one knew her and no one would bring up the divorce or that her last husband abandoned her because he was gay. This meant, however, that she no longer lived near Maria or Daniel or Jose Luis. But she was not looking backwards anymore and wanted a new beginning. She took Michael with her because he was still young and underage. But eventually, a month or so later, her oldest son, Jose Luis, moved in with them when he also lost his job.

It was not the first time Lucia moved away to avoid past hurts. She moved away from Chambers Lane after Daniel turned eighteen, graduated from high school, and he moved away to attend college. Daniel was the last of the three children that Lucia had from her first marriage with Jose Luis Mendoza. She hoped that moving into the small two-bedroom mobile home in Canyon Country would mean that the two eldest children, Maria and Jose Luis, would finally move out as well. She made them pay rent and even raised it twice in hopes to get them to move out when they turned eighteen, but they refused to do so and preferred the security of living with their mother even if it meant paying higher rent. Their constant bickering and fighting caused her so much stress that she finally decided to seek professional counseling on top of the religious counseling that her local pastor provided. Her therapist advised her to move away;

otherwise the stress would kill her. In some ways, maybe she was still following that advice when she decided to move to Georgia to avoid the stress of her divorce from Michael's father.

"Lucy!! Is that you?"

She shyly raised her head and responded, "Yes, Pastor Brown," and quietly wiped the remaining tears from her face.

"What's wrong?"

"My, my son, ... Michael. He's dead."

Pastor Brown approached Lucia and sat next to her, wrapped his arm around her shoulder, and began to silently pray for Michael. Lucia mustered the strength to silently pray as well.

"Thank you, Pastor," Lucia said when he finished. She became teary-eyed again.

"Michael was a lovely boy. He hadn't come to church in awhile. But I remember you mentioning him during prayer meetings every week and praying for him. We all did."

"I always appreciated that Pastor." The church had always been a family to her during hard times, even when Sylvia and her husband were having difficulties.

"We are all here for you, Lucy. Is there anything that you need?"

"I don't know what I am going to do without him," she sobbed. "He was my baby."

"The Lord will be there to comfort you, Lucia. You need to just trust in Him and His plan for you."

"I will try, Pastor."

They began to speak of Michael's passing and Pastor Brown offered to perform a memorial at the church. Lucia was happy about the offer, but did not want to bury Michael in Georgia. They had only lived there a few years and Michael disliked it there. He often complained that he felt even more estranged in Georgia as a biracial boy. The white kids in school and in church were almost as pale as Michael was, but he seemed to tan easier and not burn. The kids wondered why. It was the Puerto Rican side of him that would make it easier for him to tan quickly. Lucia's friends were all Caucasians. She even mistakenly forgot that she was not white at times. Michael, however, did not have the same experience. The white kids would make racial remarks about him and his mom and would cruelly tease him that he would become gay like his father. The black kids considered him white and wanted nothing to do with him.

But what ultimately made Michael feel betrayed and unloved was when the young, white teenage girl from his high school that he had fallen in love with, Sally, would not accept him because he was biracial and not truly white in her eyes. At times, she enjoyed his wanton desire to spend time with her and was flattered by it, but she adamantly refused to go on any dates with him or even be seen with him at school at least around other kids. What would her parents think if she brought a black boy home; even though Michael was actually half Puerto Rican and not half black? That didn't matter to Sally's parents because his curly hair gave away his racial impurities and she knew it. She told Michael this when his persistent begging to go out with her finally annoyed her so, especially after the other kids noticed that Michael was attracted to her. This rejection pained Michael so much that he longed to move back to California. He was a California boy at heart and he sported a "Cali-boy" tattoo on his right forearm as a badge of honor that he frequently showed to people to reassure them that he indeed belonged somewhere. At least that is what he told himself when he was home alone.

After that, month after month, he would beg his mother to move back to California where most of his friends and siblings were. Lucia assured him that they would move back soon, but on her own terms. She proudly rejected any assistance from her family that meant they would have to move in with a family member until she could get on her feet. She would only move back if she could afford to buy another home like the one she sold five years ago before moving to Georgia. The family advised her against such a requirement because in the intervening years, home prices in California had skyrocketed and Lucia's salary in Georgia was actually less than what she had earned as a certified nursing assistant in California. There was no way that she could afford to buy a house before moving back and she did not have any savings to accomplish it. The family considered this unattainable condition as just a way to deflect and to avoid admitting that Lucia did not want to move back to California or to avoid admitting that she moved back in defeat. The more she stood her ground; the more despondent Michael became until he lost all hope that they would ever move back to California and that he would never again feel acceptance like he did when he was younger.

What deepened Michael's despondency was his knowledge that remaining in Georgia would only reaffirm his belief that his mother wanted to stay closer to Sylvia and her children. Lucia made no qualms that her favorite child was Sylvia, although she would deny it if asked. Sylvia was her love child with Marcelo. Though she cared deeply for Michael's father initially, his betrayal inevitably affected her affections for Michael even if he was the youngest. Surprisingly, Marcelo's betrayal never had the same effect on Lucia's feelings toward Sylvia. Lucia doted on Sylvia and her other kids knew it. Sylvia was given the best gifts for Christmas, made special meals even if it wasn't a holiday or her birthday, or was given any money that Sylvia asked for even if Lucia did not have the money or Lucia had to give Sylvia money that she had saved for one of the other kids in order to satisfy Sylvia's insatiable need for money. When the other kids learned of these sacrifices, Lucia would deny it and make excuses why a birthday gift or a wedding gift was missing or smaller than expected or promised. Now that Sylvia had kids of her own and Lucia lived in a rented house next door in Marietta, she could shower her grandkids with the same love and affection that she showed Sylvia. Lucia's other kids eventually accepted that except Michael. Now that he realized that his mother would not move back to California, he became obsessed with the idea that his mother really did not love him and that his siblings did not love him either.

With these muddled thoughts swirling in her head, Lucia finally told Pastor Brown as she sat in the sanctuary of the church hoping the Lord would guide her and help her decide where to bury Michael.

"I don't think Michael would want to be buried in Georgia."

"Why?"

"He hated it here. The best time of his life was when he was a child growing up in Canyon Country. I want to remember him always like that."

"So what are you going to do?"

"I think I want to bury him in California. That way his brothers and sisters and cousins can visit him. If he is buried here, then the rest of the family wouldn't be able to visit him."

At that moment, Lucia realized what else she needed to do. She needed to swallow her pride and move back to California even if it meant living with a relative. Perhaps, Maria would offer her home and maybe her mother would pay for the flight to California.

"But wouldn't that mean that you won't be able to see him if he is buried in California?"

"I've made up my mind, Pastor. I think the Lord is showing me that I need to move back to California. I can't keep living in that house. It only reminds me of Michael. I can't sleep and it is making me nervous and anxious."

"Well, if that is where He is directing you to go, then you need to follow His will."

They decided to have a wake at the church in Marietta and to take up an offering to help Lucia raise the money to fly Michael's body to California. Lucia was pleased by this. She adored the congregation and appreciated the emotional and spiritual support they provided her over the years, especially helping her get over the rejection she felt after Michael's father abandoned her.

"*It would be a happy time,*" she thought to herself. "*A time for all of them to remember Michael the way that I do.*" He would always be the small, little boy that she remembered carrying in her arms as she walked from the car to her home, despite her struggle to carry him because he was so heavy for his age.

Chapter Three

Daniel

The elevator door opened to a marble and dark cherry wood lobby with a platinum-plated plaque indicating that the law firm occupied the entire fifteenth floor of the Dial building in midtown Phoenix north of the I-10 interstate. To the right of the elevator bay was the luxuriously decorated reception area that welcomed guests and staff alike. With spatial views of Piestewa Peak and Camelback mountain to the slight northeast and downtown to the south, one could almost see the entire valley from the various windows of the fifteenth floor. But from the reception area, the looming landmark was the Sandra Day O'Connor courthouse housing the federal courts with its six-floor, glassed-enclosed atrium that nearly encompassed the entire length of the north side of the building. An older woman who hailed from North Dakota with her natural long, blond hair and off-blue eyes sat stoically at the receptionist desk in the lobby awaiting any visitors or staff that exited the elevators. She also answered any calls received at the front desk.

"Good morning, Cheryl."

"Good morning, Daniel."

It was his daily routine after arriving at the firm around 9 a.m. every morning to first greet the receptionist, grab a bottle of orange juice from the merchandizing refrigerator in the east kitchenette which was stocked full of sodas and juices of every type, including mineral and spring water. Daniel would then walk to his office past his secretary, Lori. He never greeted Lori until after he drank his morning juice, checked his email, and then checked his snail mail which Lori processed every day. One could call it a routine, but hardly precise because Daniel Mendoza, although always early or on time, was not regimented and could care less if he arrived precisely at nine or one minute after or even ten minutes after so long as it was nine-ish. This day was a slightly different day because, unbeknownst to Daniel, when he went to pick up his mail, he learned that two of the shareholders wanted to speak with him this morning. They had left a message with Lori to that effect. Daniel had no idea that such a request was waiting for him that morning and it was unusual for the shareholders to meet with associate attorneys like Daniel. Daniel usually went about his day working his cases. He rarely interacted with any of the shareholders unless he needed their approval or needed their advice on a case.

Before heading to the conference room for the meeting, Daniel decided to stop by the bathroom to freshen up to prepare for what awaited. His navy blue, pin-stripped double-breasted suit was tight fitting and slightly crumby, but his dark blue paisley tie with light pink, diagonal stripes still gave him a slight sophisticated look that he had hoped would give off an air of confidence. Luckily, Daniel had recently visited the barbershop so his dark brown hair laid down in naturally, long wavy curls reminiscent of an inverted "s", rather than the tight "o"-shaped curls that he had when his hair grew in length. The scent of Creed's Virgin Island Water vaguely wafted from his clothing. He made sure that the blue and silver oval cufflinks were properly fastened. He polished his shoes with the electric shoe buffer that was stored in the men's bathroom on the opposite side of the office away from the guest bathrooms. Daniel stood at only five foot ten inches. He hoped that his Salvatore Ferragamos with their two inch heels would give him some extra height so that he would appear taller in stature during the meeting with the shareholders. He cleaned his semi-rimless Oakley prescription glasses to remove any smudges from his fingers that would inadvertently appear when he often removed his glasses to read the various pleadings or deposition transcriptions or emails throughout the day. Daniel wanted to see clearly and wanted the shareholders to be able to look him in the eyes.

He walked slowly to the main conference room on the south side of the fifteen floor and sat down on one of the black leather chairs encircling the 14-foot long table with its Giallo Veneziano granite and cherry-wood table top that dominated the room. Cheryl had prepared the conference room like she usually did when it is reserved in advance with the typical carafe of Starbucks coffee and a pitcher of iced water. A trio of glass canisters with candy, chips, and other snacks were located adjacent to the refreshments. Nothing seemed out of place or unfamiliar to Daniel.

Bill and Tim were already there awaiting his presence. They sat on the opposite side of the table facing the door, while Daniel sat on a chair facing the southern windows where he could see the federal courthouse in the distance. They politely greeted him and shook his hand as he sat down. They offered him some refreshments, but he eagerly declined.

"Welcome. It's good to see you, Daniel. We don't get to spend as much time together because you are in court a lot," Bill said because he was the managing partner at the firm. Bill and Daniel began working a lot together in recent years. Bill had a varied past and had worked as a firefighter and volunteered as a police officer before going to law school. His voice and demeanor reflected this.

"We have a couple of things that we wanted to talk to you about now that it is near the end of August," Tim interrupted. "As you know, this is your eighth year with the firm so you are up for shareholder. We wanted to discuss some things with you about what is going to happen in the next several months before the shareholders vote on whether to extend an offer to you."

Daniel silently listened. Of the two, he knew that Tim was the more gentler attorney and had the type of personality that went along with everyone and was very friendly. He rarely, if ever, got upset, but his wife, Lisa, would always claim during the firm dinners that Tim would lose his temper at home a lot. No one really believed her. Daniel was simply glad that Richard, the other shareholder, was not a part of the meeting. Richard claimed to be a Christian, but was ruthlessly unsympathetic and selfish when it came to office politics and greedy when it came to money.

"We want to assure you that you did an excellent job this past year. Although we always appreciated your high billable hours, as we explained, this is a boutique firm and we pride ourself in the quality of life that we offer our associates and staff. We are pleased that you have lowered your hours and are focusing on other things besides work and that you are investing time in nurturing your relationships with the attorneys and staff in the firm." Bill recounted this same philosophy that he and Tim said earlier in the year about how a happy employee who is not overly stressed and overworked is not only more productive, but also less prone to make mistakes and less prone to commit malpractice. Malpractice could be financially devastating to the firm and its national reputation.

At first, Daniel was focused solely on work and dreaded the shareholders' advice two years ago that he needed to spend time every morning listening to his secretary and complimenting her more when she did things for him. His initial resentment faded and he learned to appreciate her morning stories about her daughter graduating from high school and going to college or her husband, Tommy, who worked as a computer programmer and played saxophone in a jazz band on the weekends. Daniel would never discuss anything in his own personal life with Lori. He would nod and smile and say something or another about the story Lori was sharing. She seemed to gleefully appreciate it.

Daniel was pleased to hear that the shareholders still had faith in him and acknowledged his efforts not only as an attorney, but also in creating stronger social relationships in the firm. He knew this was a good sign that he would likely get offered a partnership at the end of the year like every other senior associate who had worked at the firm. But he did not want to seem overly cocky or arrogant for fear that it might cause an unforeseen ripple that would unexpectedly impact his ability to become a shareholder. He would be the first Hispanic attorney in the firm's long history. Daniel knew that there were very few Hispanic attorneys in town and very few who made shareholder at a prestigious firm.

He had worked very hard all of these years as an attorney after graduating summa cum laude from the Arizona State University School of Law. It wasn't known as the Sandra Day O'Connor School of Law at the time. As one of two Hispanics who graduated in the top ten percent of his graduating class, Daniel could have worked for a large firm in Phoenix and made substantially more money. He decided against working for a large firm because he wanted a better quality of life and did not want to be forced to work until 10 p.m. or later every night and work every weekend to meet a horrendous billable hour requirement. Law school had taken its toll on him, both physically and emotionally, and Daniel never wanted to endure that unbearable strain again.

To graduate with honors, Daniel studied long hours into the night and every weekend for three years. He also had to study during the holidays, especially every Thanksgiving because Winter finals began shortly thereafter. He did not mind studying long hours because he really enjoyed studying the law. In later years, he realized that he loved studying the law even more than practicing law as an attorney. What he regretted about law school was the lack of social time there was compared to undergrad and being away from his family and friends. In undergrad, Daniel was involved with his fraternity house, participated in intramural sports, watched college football, basketball, baseball, and volleyball games, and even participated in Spring Sing and the Mardi Gras festival. Then there were the late-night dinner runs to Chinatown or Koreantown or J-town; not to mention the burger runs to Fatburgers or Tommy Burgers or In-N-Out. But law school was different. Daniel focused mainly on studying with very little extracurricular activities except the one time that he attended the Fiesta Bowl during his second year.

Daniel was not very close to his family. He welcomed the move from Los Angeles to Phoenix because he knew that it would give him the space to live his own life without being smothered by family obligations or the never-ending drama that seemed to plague the Mendoza family. A part of him still wanted to visit his family on occasion. Moving to Arizona to attend law school made that almost impractical. What made things even worse was that all the rest of his college friends from undergrad were married and began starting their families around the time that Daniel moved to Phoenix and began law school. His college friends no longer had time to spend nights with Daniel like they used to; whether that was going to dinner, a concert, or just to the movies. Could he blame them? They had responsibilities now that he did not share and in some ways could not fully understand. It made spending nights alone studying all the more bearable because he could rationalize that all of his college friends lived out of state and were too busy nonetheless. He made fewer friends in law school compared to undergrad. It wasn't as easy making friends in law school compared to undergrad because he was not from Arizona. A lot of Daniel's law school classmates were married with young kids and had very little time to socialize given their rigorous study schedule. So he found solace in studying alone, but all the while Daniel hoped to find someone special in his life. It was especially difficult to find a young attractive, Hispanic female who had the same education and shared the same conservative values as Daniel, even though there was a large Hispanic population in the greater Phoenix metropolitan area.

Daniel's mother never taught her children how to speak Spanish. She seemed to think it was a hindrance to their new lives in Los Angeles. Los Angeles was far away from where she was born in Rio Piedras, Puerto Rico - a small suburb of San Juan where the university was located. Perhaps, if Daniel was born in Rio Piedras, then he may have attended the University of Puerto Rico and would have met other female Puerto Ricans and married one. Perhaps, he could have grown up knowing and speaking Spanish the way Puerto Ricans do - fast and with a Caribbean dialect peppered with Taino or African words like mofongo and gandul. Maybe he could have fit in more if his grandmother never moved to the States in the 30s. To those Puerto Ricans living on the island, Daniel was not a true Boricua because he could not speak the language and did not really know the struggles and culture of his people.

Living on Chambers Lane, there were no other Puerto Ricans and only one or two Hispanic families in that part of town. A Mexican family lived caddy-cornered from the Mendoza family home. They were an elderly couple whose children moved away, but who were raising their grandson, Jesse. Jesse was five years Daniel's junior. Another Mexican family lived around the corner from Chambers Lane. Other than these two families, every other family in the neighborhood was white and primarily elderly. Very few kids lived on that street. There were even fewer Hispanic kids who went to the same elementary school, middle school, and high school that Daniel would attend that could speak Spanish. What need did Daniel and his other siblings have for Spanish? There was no one that they could talk to in Spanish. Their mother spoke perfect English even though her first language was Spanish. When she was younger, Lucia Mendoza Sheffield worked as an ESL teacher's assistant at the local elementary school teaching Spanish-speaking students both English and Spanish. But the only time she spoke Spanish in front of the Mendoza children was when she was speaking to her mother or to her siblings.

Lucia's mother could not really speak English that well. Isabel and Belén could speak English just as well as their younger sister Lucia. Surprisingly, they all lacked a Puerto Rican accent when speaking English. Daniel opined that his mother preferred speaking to her siblings and mother in Spanish so that Daniel and the other kids could not understand what they were saying. The end result was that Daniel could understand a lot more Spanish, more than he could speak it or read and write it. He had trouble formulating sentences in Spanish. Because Daniel really did not know anyone who did speak Spanish besides his family, he did not mind any inability to coherently speak it. Trying to speak Spanish only highlighted his shortcomings.

Finding a good Hispanic woman in Arizona who could understand that Daniel could not speak Spanish and never really spoke Spanglish was difficult. Finding a Puerto Rican woman to marry was impossible. Daniel was an anomaly among the Hispanic community and never really felt that he fit in. He was unable to speak to any of his dating prospects in Spanish or to their parents or grandparents. The family of most of his prospects recently immigrated from Mexico or some other Latin America country. Consequently, more than likely they did not speak English well or at all. They considered Daniel's inability to speak Spanish as an explicit rejection of his Hispanic culture and believed that it proved that Daniel had an air of superiority that echoed his intelligence. As a result, his female prospects were discouraged by their families from pursuing a relationship with Daniel and frequently mentioned that to him. In the end, Daniel decided to vigorously pursue his education and career rather than a relationship or a family, which he thought from prior experiences would inevitably be short lived.

What made matters worse was that, although Daniel was raised Catholic since he was a baby, was baptized, attended catechism classes on Sunday at the local church, and was confirmed in his early teens, he never really accepted the Catholic faith with its Virgin Mary and many saints and rigid religious observance. Instead, he converted to Protestantism shortly after he turned eighteen and never again attended Catholic Church. As a result, he was ostracized by his entire family and this difference also distanced him from most prospective dates. With his new found religion, he was given new restrictions different from before. There was the no-drinking-and-dancing rules, no kissing or sex until marriage, no television or movies or non-Christian songs. No dating non-Christians including even practicing Catholics or those who attended Christian cults. Everything was tightly regulated in ways that did not seem to matter to him: Wednesday night bible studies, Friday night evangelism, Sunday morning and evening services. Then there was the daily reading of the bible and prayers of salvation for his family, friends, co-workers, and the many unnamed strangers that he meet along the way. But as is typical, once the newness wore off and the myriad trials of college and family and living on his own continued, his commitment waned.

As Daniel sat in the conference room on the fifteenth floor, these thoughts muddled his mind while the shareholders spoke to him. Was the sacrifice worth it? Were the rewards of possibly earning more money and more prestige from being a shareholder worth not having a wife or kids or seemingly being misplaced all these years? He was unable to answer those questions at the moment. But when Bill and Tim rose to dismiss him from the meeting, he politely thanked them and gave them the impression that it was. Maybe he still believed it at the time.

Daniel quickly walked back to his office. Although he was happy about the morning's news, something had been on his mind that entire morning and throughout the meeting with the shareholders. Now that the meeting was over, he was free to pursue what was hindering his thoughts. He decided to avoid immediately working on his cases as was his usual routine, but to instead resolve what was on his mind. If he did not, then he would always regret it for the rest of his life. He picked up the receiver in his office and then dialed.

"Mom. It's me, Daniel."

"Hi. What's wrong?" Lucia knew that something was wrong because Daniel never called his mother unless it was her birthday or a holiday. It was late August so his call was unexpected.

"Have you spoken to Junior?" Given the urgency on his mind, Daniel decided to skip the niceties and get straight to the point.

"No."

"When was the last time that you spoke to him?"

"You know how he is. He gets into these moods where he avoids the family and doesn't call. I don't think that I have heard from him in two months. He is probably still mad at me for telling him to stop fawning over Remedy and to leave that girl alone. He hasn't called me since."

Daniel began to worry. He dared not tell his mother of the dream that he had the night before that Junior had died.

"I tried calling his cell, but he didn't answer or return my calls."

"Did you call Maria and ask her if she has spoken with him?"

"Not yet. I'll do that now."

Daniel quickly got off the phone without saying goodbye and frantically dialed his sister's telephone number. He misdialed several times until he told himself to calm down, relax, and focus on dialing. The phone rang, but he was sent to voicemail.

"Maria, it's me, Daniel. Have you spoken to Junior? I'm looking for him. If you speak to him, tell him to call me immediately. Thanks." He hung up and dialed another number.

"Sylvia, can you hear me?"

Her voice came in and out due to a bad connection until Daniel could finally hear Sylvia repeatedly saying "Hello!" When the connection cleared, Daniel could hear her kids complaining about the problems with the video game console and their inability to continue playing. They were fighting as usual, which he noticed they fought every time he was on the phone with Sylvia.

"Hold on," Sylvia said. Daniel could hear Sylvia's frustrated voice saying "I told you, Christine, not to play with Bernardo. You know he gets angry when he loses."

Daniel impatiently waited for Sylvia to handle the situation and get back on the phone.

"These kids never listen to me and wonder why everything breaks down."

Daniel knew the routine and that he had to endure several minutes where his younger sister who would first have to voice her worries about the kids, her husband, and then her various jobs before she would remember that Daniel must have called her for a reason.

"So what's up?", Sylvia finally asked.

"I was wondering if you have spoken to Junior lately."

"That fool. That dude is so cheap. He had the nerve to avoid me when I asked him if he could send me some money to buy the kids some crayons for school. He always wants money from people. Just six months ago, I gave him a hundred dollars to get his California driver's license. You would think that he could at least send me five dollars for my kids after all that I've done for him."

"You know it doesn't cost a hundred dollars to get a license."

"I know. I know." Sylvia's voice was tepid yet surprisingly firm.

"Junior is like that. He likes scamming people out of money. He gets a weird sense of pride out of it and brags about it to everyone. But he gets irate if you ask for money or if you ask him to repay you. That's why I never give him any money because he never pays it back." Daniel was dumbfounded that he had to explain his older brother's actions to Sylvia. She readily knew this about Jose Luis.

"I haven't heard from Junior since he wouldn't give me the money for the crayons. I'm tired of chasing after that kid…"

Sylvia continued on until Daniel realized that she had no information to give other than her uncontrollably outbursts of anger and regret. He kept listening until she exhausted herself from it and the conversation naturally ended. Daniel reminded Sylvia to have Jose Luis call him, but he doubted that she would remember to do so even if Jose Luis immediately called after Daniel hung up. She was forgetful like that.

Being desperate, Daniel thought that he should call his cousins because they would sometimes hang out with Jose Luis and smoke marijuana together. After calling Raymond, Carlitos, Theresa, Cynthia, and Marisol, none of them answered so he left each of them a voicemail message. He dared not call his cousins from his Aunt Isabel's side of the family. Besides, he knew that they all avoided Jose Luis like the plague because of his incessant drug use. Only his cousin Donnie, who also engaged in marijuana, had any contact with Jose Luis. But Donnie lived in Michigan near his estranged wife and unlikely had knowledge of Jose Luis's whereabouts. So Daniel did not call him either.

After leaving the various voicemail messages, Daniel sat down at his desk and tried to concentrate on his dream while trying not to become anxious. The dream had become hazier as time passed. But Daniel could still see his brother's body encapsulated in a white vinyl body bag with a Manila ID tag containing Jose Luis's scribbled name that was barely legible in blue ink as if written by a very elderly man. His personal effects were inside a ziplock pouch. Jose Luis's glib face peeked through the small opening just enough for Daniel to discern that his older brother was in fact inside. The dankness was excruciating and heavy, but inescapable. A serene feeling plagued the dream in a way that Daniel could not understand. But Daniel saw himself approaching the bag as if to entirely open it when the haziness of the dream faded into an indiscernible blur. Daniel could no longer remember any more of the dream despite his numerous efforts to recall more.

The brothers had never been close except that summer of his senior year when Jose Luis temporarily enlisted into the Army and they shared dreams of his future together. After he was honorably discharged and returned home a few weeks later after starting boot camp, Jose Luis knew that Daniel was disappointed. Inevitably, the temporary rift subsided and the two discussed what happened and how this effected Jose Luis's future. The relationship really was never the same again. Jose Luis would call Daniel periodically over the years and complain for hours on the phone. Daniel, however, could walk away from the phone and would do other things because Jose Luis would simply talk unendingly about himself and his issues and never really asked Daniel about himself or cared what was happening in his life. Daniel never shared any of his own personal feelings or issues with his brother because any attempts were met with efforts by Jose Luis to redirect the conversation back to himself. There were years when the brothers rarely spoke and years when they spoke on a weekly basis. Because the two had not recently talked to each other in years, Daniel was surprised at the urgency that he felt to contact his brother after experiencing the dream. Daniel was also surprised at his inescapable desire to ensure that Jose Luis was still alive.

When the phone rang and Jose Luis was on the other line, Daniel was relieved. He feigned a reason for wanting to contact his brother and never admitted that the true reason was his recent dream that Jose Luis had died. The brothers talked for hours, but in fact Daniel merely listened as always and occasionally said "yes" or "no" as the conversation endlessly continued. After the conversation ended, Daniel began working on his litigation cases while at work and continued revising a motion for summary judgment that one of the newer, younger associates originally drafted.

He finished the long day at work and drove the forty-five minutes from mid-town to his home in Arrowhead Ranch. As he was removing his jacket and kicking off his shoes, Daniel heard his phone ring. The last thing he wanted to do was speak to anyone after the long day that he had, but he checked the caller ID on his phone and saw that it was Maria who was returning his call.

"Hey Maria," he said as he pushed the speaker button and continued to change into his comfortable, evening clothes that he wore around the house because no one else lived with him.

"I heard that you've been calling every one asking for Junior. I got your message."

"Yeah, he called me earlier today."

"I'm glad that you got a hold of him."

"I was worried about him because I had a dream that he was dead and I wanted to make sure that he was ok."

Maria was the only person Daniel was willing to open up to and tell the truth as to why he was frantically trying to get a hold of Jose Luis. They had become closer after his first year in law school after some personal issues arose with Maria's husband. Unlike when they were teenagers when they rarely spoke to each other, the incident allowed them to finally share their thoughts and failures. After that, they spoke on a weekly basis and sometimes several times a day. So Daniel felt comfortable sharing and knew that, if he had not opened up and told the truth, Maria would ask him herself and would persistently pursue it until Daniel relented.

"What!! When did you dream that?" Maria was sometimes into dreams and signs, but she was not into astrology or numerology, tarot cards, or other sundry beliefs. So she was excited to hear that Daniel was sharing one of his dreams.

"Last night."

"Tell me about it."

"It's no big deal. Besides, it's obviously not true because he is still alive."

"You sound disappointed."

"Disappointed that he is alive or disappointed that the dream is not true?"

"Whatever. You know what I mean."

The siblings continued into the evening discussing Daniel's dreams and the various dreams that Maria had over the years and their meanings until Daniel had to end the conversation to begin cooking dinner.

"I'll call you later, Maria. I have so much to do."

He expected to hear from Maria on Friday night when her husband typically worked late and when she felt lonely and had no one to talk to. When the phone rang unexpectedly early the next morning and Maria called to tell him that their younger brother Michael was dead, Daniel was overwhelmed with guilt. At no time did Daniel every think to call Michael or to consider that his dream wasn't really about his older brother Jose Luis, but was about Michael. Michael and Daniel were never close. After he graduated from college, Daniel temporarily lived at home with his mom and Michael, who was only two years old at the time. Because Daniel was twenty-three years his senior, he never really felt close to Michael and in some ways, may have never considered him his brother or felt like they were related. After Daniel moved out of his mom's house, he rarely saw Michael in the intervening years, but heard stories about him from his mom and Maria. It only made him feel even more distant from Michael.

Chapter Four

Maria

From the dining room table, one could see through the dusty, large bay windows into the backyard and notice the brown, dying grass; in some places overgrown with crabgrass and in others with ragweed. It was as if the lawn had been neglected for months and perhaps years and never mowed. The sprinklers were turned off not because of water conservation due to the ongoing drought, but because of the indolence of the supposed male head of household. Dandelions also grew among the drought-tolerate plants such as poppy mallow with their magenta flowers that no longer bloomed, or among the lavender and grey santolina that grew in rows along the slowly dilapidating wooden fence, and also among a host of purple and yellow lantana. Small, brown desert ants walked in a meandering path looking for food; their bulbous gasters and venomous stings at the ready. Fecal matter from the numerous family dogs were decaying as if the household residents never looked after their pets and never cleaned up after them. Its odor (commingled with that of canine urine) scented parts of the backyard, but the residents were apparently oblivious to it. It was evident that the residents never really utilized their backyard. There were no barbecue cookouts for the Fourth of July or Labor Day weekends. No one sunbathed outside during the warm winter months of the high desert and no one read a book outside alone accompanied by tall glasses of homemade sweet tea at the ready when refreshments were needed. Although the yard was big enough to build a spacious in-ground pool and still had plenty of room for entertaining guests, the owners never built one despite owning the home for nearly a decade and repeatedly assuring family and friends that someday one would be built.

In stark contrast to the bleak and grotesque backyard, the dining room table was adorned with Cambrian stoneware place sets rendered in a soft burgundy cream palette with rustic brown; reminiscent of old-world charms. First, there was the service plate embossed with graceful, burgundy-colored vines. On top of the service plate was the smaller dinner plate with a similar pattern and then a soup bowl and an accompanying stone mug. Each of the six place settings were encircled with a smaller than normal array of utensils: a dinner knife and soup spoon on the right and a salad fork and dinner fork on the left. Accompanying the mug on the upper right was a water goblet and a wine glass. To the upper left, a butter plate with a butter knife diagonally laid on top. The beige napkin was folded into a standing fan. Originally, the place settings were dusted regularly and ceremoniously ever day. But over time even this waned. Specs of dust were visible more now than ever, betraying that the owners really never used them and that they were simply for decoration.

At the table sat Maria Jane Mendoza-Flores. She was short and stout. A younger version of her mother, Lucia. She no longer wore her black hair long with bangs the way she did for decades in high school and in elementary school. Instead, she wore an unstructured bob with plunging sides that mysteriously still gave her hair a sense of volume, but which she liked because it was easy to maintain and easy to put into a bun when she needed to go to work or leave the house to run errands, but did not have the time to upkeep her hair. This was surprising given that the bob revealed more of her neck than she typically did; giving her an air of confidence she never really had since the accident.

She was twenty when she was driving in her car with her then boyfriend, Roberto, and her young daughter. She was driving to one of the many undisclosed places they would hang out. Two cars were racing recklessly on the freeway, weaving in and out of traffic. One of the racing cars cut in front of an eighteen-wheeler, causing it to swerve into the next lane and striking Maria's blue MG causing it to spin out of control down the freeway. Maria had recently purchased the MG from Marcelo. The kinetic energy from the accident caused Maria to be thrown from the vehicle, but her boyfriend and her daughter were still inside. Maria slid down the black, asphalt highway. She had second and third degree burns all along her back and some along the back of her neck. Roberto pulled out the young girl right before the car caught on fire as Maria watched from afar writhing in pain. It took Maria six months to recover in the burn ward.

That near death experience left Maria confused. Afterwards, she wanted to live life to the fullest, never really knowing when it could end. She also struggled with the uncertainty of the afterlife and wanting to ensure a place there. The dichotomy of her character was evident and most individuals were confounded by her two extremes which shifted from year to year, if not day to day. She covered any inner anger and despair the same way she covered the keloids on her neck with fluffy, big collars and oftentimes with her hair. No one could see either external or internal wounds. Now in her mid-forties, the scars no longer mattered. She no longer hid them from her husband or anyone else who she encountered. Her new bob was a coming out of sorts.

At the dining room table, Maria was nervously inputting information for her daily route for her merchandising job into her tablet so that she could sync it with her personal computer and then upload the data to her company's server. Without this step, she would not be paid her hourly rate nor paid for the miles she drove with her personal car. She would drive her personal car to various locations to restock DVDs at local retail stores or to replace the movie posters in the display cases at the local movie theaters or to build three-dimensional cardboard movie displays. It was her daily routine to input her mileage and other information into her computer at the end of each workday.

Maria busied herself with her work in order to avoid the rush of emotions when she thought of her youngest brother, Michael. She remembered the last time that she saw him when her mother, Lucia, and Michael still lived in Perris, California. It was Thanksgiving. Lucia decided on that occasion to actually celebrate the holiday by having a dinner at her house. Normally, Lucia would visit her sisters in Compton for each and every holiday so she never celebrated holidays at her own house with her own kids. This time, Isabel and Belén actually drove to Lucia's house. Even their mother came as well as Maria and Marie, Maria's only daughter. Surprisingly, some cousins, Evelyn and Yvonne - who were recently visiting from Puerto Rico, came too.

Maria remembered the pot luck Thanksgiving that year. Instead of cooking a traditional turkey dinner, they decided to celebrate the holiday Puerto Rican-style. Maria made the Pavachon - a roasted turkey that is slow roasted the way sucking pigs are roasted on the island; seasoned with adobo, cloves of garlic, pepper, and oregano. She also stuffed the Pavachon with mofongo - mashed plantains typically combined with seafood, or various meats like pork or shrimp, or vegetables and formed into a mound. Plantains, when used as a stuffing, were typically combined with bacon, garlic, and chicken broth. That holiday, Maria had asked her mother to make her two favorites: habichuelas (red beans) and arroz con gandules (rice with pigeon peas). There was also tostones and morcilla (although it was not homemade using pig's blood and pig's intestines the way Maria's paternal grandfather still made it even though he now lived in Lamont outside of Bakersfield, California instead of the island). The morcilla was store bought, but no one cared. They all enjoyed it as if it was homemade. Isabel made her famous soul food - macaroni and cheese and greens with ham hocks. She could cook every kind of soul food, but would only bring these items when she was cooking for a party away from home. Belén made chicken mole. To drink, there was coquito which is a Puerto Rican drink similar to egg nog, but made with coconut milk instead. There were also cans of coco rico to drink and Maria's favorite, Malta India - a lightly carbonated malt beverage that is brewed from barley, hops, and water; the same way that beer is brewed. Although Maria would settle for Malta Goya or Malta El Sol if her favorite was not available.

Various music played in the background. Lucia loved 50's music. During the Thanksgiving celebration, the music played softly and sporadically in the background. You could hear Fats Domino's "Ain't That A Shame", "Chantilly Lace" by The Big Bopper, "Oh, What A Night", "Honest I Do", and a host of other songs that Lucia loved to hear while growing up. Towards the end of the evening, as usual, the music would transition to Puerto Rican salsa by Willie Colón or Celia Cruz or Ruben Blades. Inevitably, boleros, guaracha, plena, and rumba played, especially their favorite singer, Daniel Santos, whom Lucia named one of her sons after. It was said that Daniel Santos was a family relative, perhaps a second cousin, but no one really knew. They simply believed it and took it at face value. Surely, everyone on the island claimed they were related to him.

During the festivities, Michael was upstairs in his room with one of his cousins, Marcus, doing something loud. Everyone downstairs in the living room could hear the ruckus; the banging against the floor which was the ceiling for the first floor, the incessant laughing and cursing, and loud music played to mask what the boys were doing so as to avoid getting in trouble. Lucia turned to her oldest grandchild at the time, Marie, and asked her to tell Michael to lower the music so that the rest of the house did not have to hear it. Marie thought, "*He is your son. Why don't you do it yourself?*" But she silently complied.

Marie walked up the stairs to the second floor. Although Michael was only thirteen at the time and Marie was twenty-one, he was still her uncle. More importantly, Michael was taller and twice her size. She knocked on the master bedroom door, which was Michael's room. Lucia had given Michael the master bedroom on the pretext that he needed his own bathroom and no one else should have to share it with him. At the time, Lucia's oldest son, Jose Luis, also lived with her. She would rather share the secondary bathroom with Jose Luis than with Michael. That decision, however, gave Michael the false impression that he ruled the house and no one else could tell him what to do, not even his mother. He openly acted that way to everyone's chagrin.

Marie kept knocking at the door, but Michael would not answer.

"I know you are in there."

Marie had not realized that the door was not locked, but as she continued knocking, it opened slightly. As she tried to open the door wider, Michael rushed to the door to close it, almost slamming it against her. Marie was shocked by this aggression and wondered what the two were doing.

"Get out of my room!!"

"Your mother asked me to tell you to lower the music," she sternly retorted.

"I said get out of my room!!"

Michael pushed Marie backwards and she almost fell over, but the door stopped her fall and she hit the back of her head on it. Marcus looked stupidly at what was occurring and said not a word.

"What the f$#% are you doing? Get mad at your mom, not me."

Marie walked out of the room, realizing that it was not worth getting into a fight with her uncle who was twice her size. She also realized that her grandmother should be checking up on Michael, not her.

She walked downstairs and told her mom about what Michael did to her.

Maria was upset and walked over towards her mother. "Mom, Michael pushed Marie."

"Well, you know how he is."

"Are you going to do something about it? You were the one who asked Marie to tell him to lower the music."

Lucia sat there pretending to ignore her daughter. Maria noticed it and it only made her more upset.

"I hate this shit. You never discipline Michael. You could whoop Junior, Danny, and I, but you can't discipline Michael. He is worse than all of us combined and really needs whooping. What kind of mother are you?"

Maria began gathering her things and aggressively walking to the front door, "Come on Marie. Let's go." Marie followed her mom to the front door. Before reaching the door, Maria turned to her mother and said, "I want nothing to do with Michael until he apologizes to Marie."

"I can't make him do that."

"Well, I won't have anything to do with you either." She grabbed Marie's hand and said. "Let's get the hell out of here" and stormed out of the house.

No apology was forthcoming and it only made Maria even more obstinate that she wanted nothing to do with her youngest brother. He was clearly in the wrong. Her mother should have seen that and should have stepped up and sided with Marie and acted like a mother to resolve the family feud. But in Maria's eyes, her mother never acted like a mom and never intervened in her children's affairs to make things right, even when they were little children. Lucia would simply say that she would pray on it and pray for her kids. Her attitude first allowed her oldest son, Jose Luis, to be abusive to the rest of her children and now it was allowing her youngest son, Michael, to be the same way.

In remembering this Thanksgiving incident while currently sitting at her dining room table and still fiddling with her tablet to input the final information for her daily route, Maria soon remembered what happened shortly thereafter. After the Thanksgiving celebration, Maria got engaged to her boyfriend, Eduardo Flores. She was happy to finally get married for the first time although she waited to get engaged until she was forty years old. They did not have the money for a fantasy destination wedding. Most of her family and friends could not afford the airfare to Hawaii or Puerto Rico or to any other Caribbean destination where she may have wanted to get married. Maria no longer was involved in the Catholic Church and no longer believed in God at the time. So a church wedding was out of the question. She asked some of her friends who lived in the area and they all recommended having the wedding and reception at the Empire Lakes Golf Course in Rancho Cucamonga. It was an award-winning Arnold Palmer-designed course. Maria and her husband did not play golf, but they envisioned holding the wedding in front of one of the lakes that overlooked the San Reuben Mountains with the Angeles National Forest in the distance. She could then hold the reception in the large, enclosed gazebo near the clubhouse.

More importantly, when thinking about who would attend her wedding, she decided that she did not want kids to attend. She had recently attended a wedding where an infant was incessantly crying and disrupted the entire ceremony. She wanted to avoid such havoc and wanted her own wedding to be a memorial for all as well as the best day of her life.

"Marie, I was thinking of not allowing kids at my wedding," she said to her daughter one day a few weeks before the wedding.

"I love babies, but crying kids are too much. What about a cry room in the back?"

"The wedding will be held outdoors. So it is impossible to have a cry room."

"Are you going to have a specific age limit?" she inquired.

"I was thinking thirteen years old."

"Thirteen? Isn't that a little too high? Thirteen year olds aren't infants."

"I don't want unruly kids running all over the place and out of control. I don't care what age they are. It's my day and I don't want them ruining it. They can have fun at some other event for kids."

It did not immediately dawn on Marie what was the impact of her mother's decision. When it did, Marie was afraid to ask her mother. The ensuing silence was deafening.

"He hasn't apologized yet. It's been months," Maria said. She knew what her daughter was afraid to ask.

"I don't think he will ever apologize."

"He needs to. If not, then he needs to learn a lesson."

"Grandma's not going to like that. She will be mad."

"I don't care."

"What if Michael apologizes?" Marie knew that this was an impossibility.

"Your grandmother will make him apologize once she learns that he can't come to the wedding. But he won't be sincere. I know Michael. He will just mutter sorry while rolling his eyes. He's not sorry. He just doesn't want to be left alone. Oh well, too bad." Maria tried to hold back a laugh, but it inevitably snuck out. She knew Michael really did not want to go to the wedding anyway and, if invited, he would go only because his mom forced him to. But excluding him would only make Michael determined. Michael would insist to his mother that he should go to prove that he had control over the situation and that everyone had to kowtow to his every wish.

Maria announced to her family that no child thirteen and under could attend her wedding. Within the week, as expected, Michael called Maria to apologize. She would not accept it. His apology was not sincere and, frankly, no apology would have sufficed. Like her mother, once Maria set her mind to something, she was obstinate and unyielding. Michael never attended Maria's wedding. At the reception, Lucia was bitter and her face could not hide it. Her snarky remarks also revealed it.

"I want to thank everyone for coming to me and Eduardo's wedding. The photographer is going to take a picture of my entire family. Can they meet at the right for the photo?" Maria handed the microphone to the DJ, who continued to play music, and she walked to the far end of the gazebo to take the family photo.

Junior and Daniel and Marie stood up to join her. Her niece, Mariah, was there too as the flower girl. Maria paid for the airfare for Mariah and Maria's younger sister, Sylvia, so that they could both attend the wedding, but she would not pay for Sylvia's husband to come to the wedding. As the photographer took several pictures, he exclaimed, "You have a beautiful family!"

Lucia muttered under her breath with resentment, "The whole family isn't here." But everyone could hear her. Lucia did not care if they could.

Someone said, "Only those family members who count are here."

Seven years later, Michael passed away. Maria had not seen him in the interim since the Thanksgiving dinner at her mother's house. She now felt guilty about imposing a "no child" policy at her wedding and not inviting Michael to the wedding. In the end, it did not matter that he was stubborn. She regretted not forgiving him now that she could no longer fix their relationship. This haunted her, which resulted in her nervousness while inputting her work information into the tablet. Every time she typed, she misspelled a word or typed the wrong number. She knew that, by focusing on work, she was avoiding what she had agreed to do: plan Michael's funeral arrangements in California. Every time she thought of calling the funeral home, she would hang up before the call was answered. Tears welled in her eyes as the regret consumed her. She did not understand why. She typically stood strong and stoic against every challenge or obstacle since the accident and prided herself about that even if others deemed it callous and controlling. This occasion should have been no different, but it was. So she did the only thing she could think of. She put down the tablet and picked up her cellphone to call her younger brother, Daniel.

"Hello."

"Hey Danny. What are you doing?"

"Nothing. Just talking to Randy. He is in town from Oklahoma."

"That's good."

The phone was silent so Daniel knew something was wrong. Maria had not called him since she told him earlier in the week that Michael was dead. The two had texted on occasion since but not about anything serious.

"What's wrong?" Daniel asked.

"Mom knew that Michael was thinking about suicide."

"What did you say?" Daniel was stunned by this comment and wanted to make sure that he had heard Maria correctly.

"She knew that Michael wanted to commit suicide." This time she said it loud enough for Daniel to inescapably understand. He had heard it the first time, but his mind did not want to accept it.

"Are you saying mom knew?"

"Yes."

"Why didn't she tell anyone?"

"I don't know. She didn't tell me until after he died. Michael told her that he was thinking of committing suicide and she spent all night and all day with him for three days watching him so that he wouldn't do it. She couldn't take the lack of sleep anymore."

"She should have called us and let us know. Why didn't she call us?" His exasperated voice was very evident.

"She never said why."

"Did she at least tell Sylvia?"

"No."

"Why not? Sylvia lives across the street and could have talked to Michael or help mom watch him."

"You know Sylvia. If it's not about her or her husband, then she doesn't care. Besides she doesn't get along with Michael. No one does."

"Why didn't she take him to a doctor so that the doctor could prescribe Michael an anti-depressant?"

Maria had no answer, leaving Daniel desperate for the solutions that could have been done.

"Mom goes to church. Why didn't she call her pastor so he could talk to Michael? If I remember, Michael used to go to church with mom too." Daniel had other questions that he wanted to pose, but he knew that Maria was not in the mood to answer all of them.

"He hasn't gone in years," Maria explained. "I'm not sure why mom didn't tell her pastor or her church friends."

"I'm sure her church would have been willing to pray for Michael, tell him why he matters, and why he shouldn't commit suicide. They should have helped mom too so that she didn't feel like it was all on her."

Daniel proceeded to remind Maria that he had called everyone including their mother about his concerns for Jose Luis' whereabouts. Daniel knew that his real concern was that Jose Luis was dead, but failed to tell anyone that. He wondered why their mother had not told him that Michael was distraught and depressed and feeling suicidal. Anger began to slowly grow him. "Do you think mom encouraged him?"

"What do you mean?"

"She is always talking about how she wishes she was dead so that she can be with Jesus and avoid all the pain here on earth. I am just wondering if she told the same thing to Michael."

"I don't know. To be honest, I always thought Michael was going to kill her. I never thought that he would die so young."

Maria recounted all of the things that Michael did: starting fires, tormenting animals, and spraying Nazi graffiti. The two had previously talked about how these seemed like signs that Michael lacked empathy; the way serial killers did. They feared that his abusive and controlling ways would lead him to uncontrollable anger towards their mother, especially because she did not always treat him fairly and would constantly fear that he would turn out gay like his father. To Lucia, that was a sin and she feared it the worse. The other family members believed that she was simply taking out her anger on Michael because Michael's father abandoned her for a gay relationship.

"Maybe she wanted him dead," Daniel finally let out. "Maybe she was afraid of him and thought he might kill her someday and so when he thought about committing suicide, she didn't do anything to prevent it. It was her way of finally being free of him." The thought only angered him more.

Maria could not believe what Daniel was saying or thinking. Even in the back of her mind, Maria also wondered the same thing over the past few days. She felt ashamed to think of it. "Poor boy," she whispered as she began to weep at the thought. "He was all alone in Georgia having to deal with mom all by himself. You know how she can be."

Maria tried hard to avoid thinking about their childhood and what things were said or done. She also did not want to remember all of the things that she had to endure with her mother while raising Marie as a child. Maria remembered the constant comments her mother would say that no other mother would ever say if she loved her children or grandchildren. Everything was said, according to her mother, because she could not lie and sin in that way.

"We should have been there for him," Maria continued.

Daniel realized that there was nothing he could do to reassure Maria. He never seen her this way: vulnerable and hurt. She was always the older, stronger sister who acted more like their mother because she believed that their real mother was emotionally absent.

"It's okay, Maria."

"What are we going to do?" She began to sob a little more.

Daniel understood what she was alluding to. The Catholic Church had always taught that suicide was a mortal sin and that anyone who committed suicide would go to hell. He knew that the family was no longer catholic, but was uncertain whether they still held this belief. Daniel was later taught that every sin was forgivable except blasphemy of the Holy Spirit. Did that include suicide? Could one seek forgiveness from God for committing suicide? How could they if they were dead and could not repent? Daniel tried to avoid thinking about this and he certainly did not bring it up to Maria.

"We will just have to pray for mom and for Michael." Daniel knew that Maria was not a believer. He himself had fallen away from the church recently, but his thoughts still turned to this unexpectedly.

Maria finally admitted that she could not bring herself to make the funeral arrangements like she had promised their mother. Every time she tried, she could not help seeing Michael's dead body and would start crying again.

"Will you come to California, Danny, so that you can go to the funeral home and make the arrangements?"

"Sure." Daniel knew that it was rare for his older sister to ask him to do something for her so he willfully agreed. "Randy wants to know if he can come too."

Maria agreed that they could stay at her house and make the arrangements from there. After Daniel hung up the phone, he could not help wondering if the dream that he had was really about his younger brother, Michael, rather than his older brother, Jose Luis. Did his misunderstanding cause the death of Michael? Had Daniel only asked about Michael's well-being instead, perhaps his mother would have told him, and he would have been able to speak to Michael; convincing him everything was okay. Daniel was burdened with the thought that Michael would still be alive if he had not made that mistake. Daniel realized that Maria was feeling the same way and regretted that she had not called about Michael's welfare earlier.

Chapter Five

Randy

The route they would need to travel out of Phoenix, Arizona primarily includes Interstate 10 even after they reach the California-Arizona border which is delineated by the Colorado river. Blythe is to the west of the great river and Ehrenberg is to the east. But first they would have to traverse the five-lane freeway from Avondale to Goodyear and then on to Buckeye where it narrowed to two lanes and then to Tonopah and onwards until they passed Quartzsite in La Paz county. Quartzsite is a small mining town approximately ten minutes from the border where local gems and minerals are sold to tourists who flock there annually. Tourists would come, not only for the seasonal swap meets and pow wows, but also for the quaint warm, winter weather. Recreational vehicles would be parked throughout the city then. Some would even stop to see the burial place of Hi Jolly (Hadji Ali) who was involved in the experimental US

Camel Corps. A plaque on Hi Jolly's tomb still stands. The camels were strong and sturdy, but were never utilized by the military because horses were frightened by them and the camels were too difficult to manage. As a result, the camels were set free in the desert long ago. Perhaps, Randy and Daniel could still catch a rare glimpse of a camel in the wild even in this day and age when they drove past Quartzsite to Maria's house in Victorville.

But Arizonans who regularly traveled the interstate to and from California readily know that the local patrol cars often hide out on the overpasses in Quartzite hoping to catch speeding cars as they exited the freeway. Having driven that way nearly fifty times or more over the past fifteen years, Daniel was very leery of Quartzsite and would never stop there, not even to get gas. Daniel would not even stop there to recharge at a Supercharger station even if he was lucky enough to own a Tesla Model S. The local corruption was well known and discussed readily on the Internet.

As he drove on the freeway at speeds of eighty to eighty-five miles an hour, the Sonoran desert blurrily flashed by. One could still make out the velvet mesquite trees that were often adorned with yellow flowering catkins that turned into long, tan seedpods reminiscent of the legumes of a tamarind tree. The bright yellow and pea-like flowers of the Palo Verde trees were no longer present as they only appeared in Spring. Occasionally, looking out the car windows, there were organ pipe and saguaro cacti scattered on the desert floor and sometimes an ironwood bush with blueish-green leaves and shiny gray bark. They could also glimpse a crissal thrasher in the thickets and a couple of warblers and sometimes a flycatcher among the trees. The Sonoran Desert was teeming with life unlike the sand dunes of the Yuma Desert with its crescent-shaped mounds and slipfaces that form with the happenstance of the wind.

They would need to drive past the Palo Verde nuclear power plant which could barely be seen in the distance and then past the Eagletail mountains and then the New Water mountains with its distinctive Eagle Eye Arch jetting upward with its colorful hues of brown and tan. On the southern side of the New Water mountains was the Kofa National Wildlife Refuge; its bighorn sheep ruggedly climbing the steep, rocky terrain. Unfortunately, the refuge could not be seen while driving along the interstate. But that did not dissuade Daniel or Randy. They continued to enjoy the scenery and the quiet, long ride to Victorville. They simply exchanged family stories along the way.

"I'm looking forward to finally seeing mom after all these years," Randy said referring to Lucia, Daniel's mother.

Randy Brackerton was stocky and had dirty blonde hair with deep blue eyes. He often worked outdoors so he was constantly tanned in his later years. He was just one year older than Daniel, but they attended the same elementary school, Mark Twain Elementary, about one block away from where they both lived on Chambers Lane as kids. They met on the first day of school and realized that they lived near each other on the same street. They would often play together, but mainly at Randy's house because Daniel liked to get away from his house and away from his overbearing siblings. When they were older, Randy would often refer to Daniel's mother as his mom even though Randy had lived with his own mother in Oklahoma for several decades after Randy eventually moved away from Chambers Lane. His mother, Ms. Polly, and her second husband, Jack, moved back to Oklahoma after Randy's grandfather passed away. Randy was only twelve years old at the time. Randy was living with his father on Chambers Lane rather than with Ms. Polly. So Randy did not immediately move back to Oklahoma with his mother and stepfather. After Randy's father lost his job a few months later, his father decided to also move back to Oklahoma and he took Randy with him. Several years later, Randy's step-father, Jack, passed away because of a heart attack. The following year, Randy's own father passed away; leaving just Randy and his mother alone in Oklahoma. One of his sisters lived there too, but she was twenty years older than Randy and they rarely saw each other even though they lived not too far from each other. His other older sisters and brothers lived along the northern coast of California near Carmel. Randy only saw them on occasion whenever he wanted to get away from the heartland and wanted to temporarily live a coastal life and play a round of golf or two.

Years later, Randy finally married, but he and Linda never had kids. She was several years older and had two teenage boys from a previous marriage. Linda was unwilling to have any more kids with Randy, even though he wanted kids with her. After Linda took a new job in Tennessee in their second year of marriage, the marriage was doomed and they were divorced the following year. Daniel was surprised to learn that Randy had recently gotten married again. Denise was also a couple of years older than Randy, but she hailed from Fort Worth, Texas. He met her at a party when he was stationed in Texas as part of the Air Force reserves. They moved into Randy's mother house in Oklahoma City after his mother passed away.

By the time Randy married Denise, he had given up on the idea of having kids. It helped that Denise was unable to have kids of her own. She never pressed the issue. They had several poodles instead, which they treated as their own children. For fun, Randy and Denise normally would drive from Oklahoma City to Holly Lake east of Dallas near the U.S. 271 where they owned a three bedroom cabin. They would stay there with their poodles, Tiny and Chip, on long three-day weekends. Randy would cook his famous ribs or brisket or smoked bologna in his Green Egg. He and his wife would spend the day paddling on the lake in their kayaks with their poodles. They would then rest on the back porch and lazily watch the deer or raccoons fiddle in their spacious, open-ended backyard that was filled with Texas pines.

But this past weekend, Randy wanted to attend a photography conference in Phoenix. He was hoping to book a few wedding gigs for his photography business and to learn a few more professional tricks to distinguish his business. His business was losing customers who would hire amateur photographers who bought cheap digital cameras and who could often underbid professional photographers like Randy and eat away at his profitable wedding photography business. Randy traveled by himself and stayed with his cousin, Phyllis, for several days in Scottsdale and then decided to spend a couple of days with Daniel at his house in Arrowhead Ranch. It was his second day at Daniel's house when Maria's call changed their plans and Randy decided to stay longer and decided to go with Daniel to California to attend Michael's funeral. Randy also wanted to assist with the funeral arrangements if possible. Randy gave Daniel a hundred dollar bill to help pay for the casket.

"Does my mom even remember you?" Daniel retorted.

"I called her in Georgia many times. She asked who it was and I told her it's your white son from Chambers Lane." Randy laughed uncontrollably the way that people do when they think they are funny, but really are not.

"What did she say?"

"Oh, she remembered me. I guess it's that Okie accent. There ain't a lot of Okies who lived on Chambers Lane." He laughed again and this time his plump, oversized belly jiggled up and down. Daniel was surprised that Randy would even call his mother. Daniel rarely heard from his mother, but on the few occasions that they did speak, she never mentioned that Randy had called her over the years.

"I also called Maria, but she never answers and doesn't call me back."

"She has been so busy lately. I'm not surprised that she doesn't call you back. She doesn't call me back either." Daniel knew that his comment was a lie. His sister, Maria, always answered his calls and if she could not speak at the time, then she would let him know that she would call him back. Typically, that did not mean immediately. Perhaps, a day or two or three later, she would return his call. Maria also never told him that Randy was calling her too. Daniel figured that she did not really know Randy; he was Daniel's childhood friend. She probably did not want to be bothered talking to a practical stranger and did not feel like telling Randy that. Months later, Maria confirmed it when Daniel asked her about the calls. Daniel was more surprised that his mother never mentioned it.

"I spoke to Michael too a couple of times," Randy added.

Daniel was shocked and felt even more uncomfortable. Michael and Daniel never spoke on the phone; not once his entire, short life. Daniel wondered why Randy would be contacting his younger brother. Trying to restrain himself, Daniel inquired, "What did you guys talk about?"

"Well, mom told me that Michael wasn't paying attention to her and wasn't do well in school. She was worried that he didn't have a father figure. Junior ain't no good influence, smoking weed and all. She wanted me to talk to him and straighten him out. So I told him that he was like a brother to me and, if he wanted to ever talk, to feel free and call me. I told him to do well in school and go to college and that if he didn't do well that I would come down there and whoop his behind myself."

"*A brother?*" Daniel thought.

Randy had never met Michael. Michael was born ten years after Randy moved back to Oklahoma. Or so Daniel thought. To Daniel's chagrin, Randy told him how he met Michael when the family lived in Canyon Country before Lucia and Michael's father moved to Colorado. Randy would visit them when he was in California visiting his own family. He met Michael again a couple of times when Lucia owned the house in Perris. Daniel wondered why his mother never mentioned any of this. It made Daniel feel even more estranged from her and the rest of the family. Daniel only wondered what other secrets that he would learn now that family and friends would come out of the wood work to attend Michael's funeral. He even pondered whether Michael's estranged father from West Virginia would attend the funeral. "*Who knows whether he was even aware that his only son was dead?*" Daniel wondered. Daniel did not expect

Lucia to call Michael's father. It was doubtful that Lucia knew where he was or knew how to get a hold of him.

"I'm really sorry about what happened, Danny. He was a great kid. I don't know why he did that? I wish he had talked to your mom or to you or to me."

Daniel did not want to explain his dream nor the fact that he thought his mother did not do enough to get Michael either psychological or spiritual help. So he tried to change the subject.

"I've never really planned a funeral before. I really don't know what to do." Daniel was hoping that Randy would share his experience when his mother died. Daniel did not find out about her death until years later.

"Well, I really don't have no experience."

"What do you mean?"

Randy proceeded to finally tell Daniel what happened to his mother. One of the neighbors' son, whom Ms. Polly knew since he was a child, became addicted to meth. One day, he rang the doorbell to Ms. Polly's house, hoping to rob her so that he could steal money for drugs. He was high as a kite at the time. When she opened the door, he pulled a shotgun that he was hiding from behind his back and shot her point blank. She only had enough time to raise both her hands in a gesture to protect herself, but the effort was futile. She was severely injured. After she recovered in the hospital for a couple of months, her right arm was paralyzed. Ms. Polly readily forgave him like the good Christian woman that she was. She was happy to learn that he was clean and sober after serving several years in prison.

But her wounds never truly healed. Ms. Polly's health significantly declined after the incident. Even after she had months of physical therapy, Ms. Polly needed home health services because she could no longer take care of herself. Randy would help out on occasion, but his photography business kept him busy especially at night and on the weekends because he often had wedding gigs to attend. When Ms. Polly's health declined so bad, she was moved to a nursing home. Within the year, she passed away after she contracted pneumonia.

"I'm sorry to hear that Randy. I never knew that. It's sad what happened to your mom."

"Danny, I appreciate that. But I've come to terms with it years ago. Mom and I were not close. She would rather go to meetings with her Alcoholic Anonymous friends and attend their camping events. I tried to get mom to help me with my photography business when she was healthy. It would have been great to have a second pair of hands and eyes; someone who could take photos with me. I was disappointed when Linda wouldn't do it. Mom wouldn't do it either. She was too busy hanging out at the AA meetings. I told her that she didn't have to go to every meeting. She's been sober for over 40 years. I wanted to spend Thanksgiving with her at home, but she was always at an AA meeting. I'm an Okie, not an Alchie. I don't wanna spend time with them anymore. Mom dragged me to all of those silly events as a kid."

Daniel remembered the time when he and Randy were in elementary school and Randy had invited him to the Salton Sea with his family one summer. The shallow, saline lake had been abandoned for decades by then and you could see dilapidated cars and buildings near the water's edge on certain parts of the shore. It was an eerie feeling. But not too far from the Salton Sea was an RV camp with natural mineral springs. That is where Randy's family and the rest of the attendees camped out. Randy and Daniel would soak each day in the hot springs after a long day playing and riding motorcycles in the desert. Later that evening, the group would all gather around the campfire. Daniel was too young and naive to understand when the older men and women would discuss how long they were sober. The group was celebrating an elderly gentleman's "birthday." Daniel could not believe the gray-haired man was celebrating his twenty-second birthday. But he went with the flow and wished the man happy birthday all the same. Daniel did not realize until their drive to Victorville that the summer trip was really an AA camp that Ms. Polly would apparently drag Randy to every so often. Daniel could sense the subtle bitterness in Randy's voice.

"Hey, Danny. I need to use the restroom. Can we stop at a gas station?"

"Sure."

By that time, the two had been driving in California for about an hour and were near Chiriaco Summit. Daniel wished that they could have stopped at the General Patton Memorial Museum if they had the time. In addition to the various Remembrance Walls made from bricks with the engraved names of servicemen and women from World Wars I and II along with the Korean, Vietnam, and Gulf wars, the museum had a bronze statue of General George S. Patton standing on tank treads with his trusty bull terrier, Willie, at his side. Daniel thought Randy would enjoy looking at the large collection of tanks there, but he knew that they should not be entertaining themselves as if they were on vacation. Maria would be upset if she found out that Daniel stopped to have fun rather than drive straight to her house in Victorville. So he instead stopped at the Chevron gas station so that Randy could use the restroom. Afterwards, the two decided to walk across the lobby to the Frosty Freeze to eat a burger and some vanilla-flavored, soft-serve ice cream because they were hungry. It was as good a time as ever to eat something. They still had another three hours before they reached Maria's house.

While eating, Daniel proceeded to ask Randy more questions about Ms. Polly's passing and her funeral arrangements. "So did you bury her in OKC?" he asked.

"No. When Jack died, mom bought a plot in California and buried him there. She also bought a plot for herself right next to him." Randy tucked his napkin on his lap and bit into the burger.

"So you buried your mom in California. That's where we are going to bury Michael. My mother doesn't want to bury him in Georgia."

"Not exactly."

"What do you mean?"

"Well, after my mom passed away, I talked to her attorney about her estate. I didn't have the money to bury her in California. So I cremated her."

"You cremated her?! Is that what your mom wanted?" Daniel asked. "*Obviously not. She bought the plot next to her husband Jack,*" he thought to himself. Daniel waited for Randy's response.

"I'm sure she doesn't mind. I called the funeral home and they said I can sell the plot back to them."

Daniel wondered what Randy would do with Ms. Polly's ashes. "I heard that you can bury the ashes in the plot. You can save money by buying a smaller headstone," Daniel explained.

"I might do that. I might go to mom's favorite beach and spread her ashes."

"That would be nice. Which beach?"

Randy never answered.

"Where are your mom's ashes now?" Daniel asked.

"They're in the plastic bag that I received from the funeral home."

"You mean that you haven't purchased an urn for her yet. You know you can get a nice urn for about fifty dollars. I saw this really exquisite urn laced with brass and it was only a hundred and fifty dollars. It was certainly on the high end for urns. You can even order them online."

"I would like to have Denise make an urn for mom. You know she throws clay. She goes to the pottery studio once a week. I've been trying to get her to go at least two to three times a week because she is no longer working and she has so much time on her hands. She keeps saying it's too expensive. But it only costs twenty-five dollars each time and I told her that I am willing to pay for it. It's worth it to me if she's happy. I know throwing clay makes her happy. But she doesn't go nearly as often enough. She sometimes sells what she makes. Her girlfriends love her work. She gets that from her mom. Denise's mom is a retired artist. She sells her artwork at a studio in Dallas. She travels a lot and is rarely home. Denise didn't want to be an artist so she went to interior design school instead and throws clay on the side for fun. I think she can make mom a great urn that mom will be proud of..."

"Well, did you ask her to make one?"

"Not yet"

"*What are you waiting for?*" Daniel thought. Instead, he asked Randy how long had it been since Ms. Polly passed away.

"It's been about three years."

"Three years!!"

Randy sensed Daniel's disappointment. "It's just that I've had so much on my plate. I had to fix up my house and rent it out so I can move into mom's house with Denise. I really like my tenant now. He is disabled and gets Section 8 assistance. I'm willing to take less monthly rent to have the security of a tenant who will pay on time and not move out. I could have gotten about two hundred dollars more a month if I rented it at the market rate. But a Section 8 tenant is more stable. You know the government is going to pay the rent on time."

Daniel was puzzled by Randy's excuses. Ever since Randy was in the Air Force and later the reserves, he was always conservative in his political views and against government handouts. After 9/11, Randy was stationed at Tinker Air Force base and patrolled the base with the other MPs. It was not like being stationed in Iraq or Afghanistan, but Randy was proud of his service, especially because it allowed him to live at home and spend time with Denise and go to the lake on weekends. Randy would always wax poetic about how he would eventually be transferred to the Ali Al Salem Air Base in Kuwait City because the U.S. also supervised the base. Dubbed "The Rock" because of its elevated position above the desert plains, Randy would frequently recount his buddies' involvement in "Operation Southern Watch." The base was very close to the Iraqi border and the servicemen and women stationed there provided various operational support such as theatre airlift, air surveillance and control, force protection, combat rescue, aero medical evacuation, and a host of others. Had Randy been stationed there, he would have provided security for convoys bringing supplies into Iraq. His bum knees made it difficult to pass the physical. Luckily, he was friends with a full bird colonel who pulled some strings to get him stationed at Tinker. Nevertheless, in the back of his mind, Randy convinced himself that he too served at The Rock. His nagging conscious encouraged him to make that thought a reality. Denise's insistence that he should stay in the States and look after his photography business was the primary reason that Randy told people why he did not serve abroad. Randy never mentioned the bum knees.

Daniel thought that Randy's military background would encourage him to give Ms. Polly a proper burial, especially because she had already purchased the plot. Daniel wondered if the monetary reasons alone were the justification. Daniel also wondered whether his mother, Lucia, would allow Michael to be cremated. This would alleviate the family's financial concerns about burying Michael. His mother did not have the money to bury him because Michael's death was so sudden. The family was trying to collect money from friends and relatives and even the church that Lucia attended. But Daniel knew that his mother's religious beliefs would never allow her to cremate her youngest son. Lucia believed in the resurrection of the body and believed that a cremated body would not rise again on the Last Day at Christ's return. Any mention of cremation would bring forth his mother's wrath and spoil everyone's mood. She would likely object to any suggestion by Daniel and would also call each of her children and siblings to dissuade anyone from supporting that suggestion. Only Jose Luis would probably not object. But that was only because he could care less about any external rituals and he knew that he would not be contributing financially to Michael's funeral anyways. Daniel knew from past experiences that it was not worth bringing it up with his mother and quickly dismissed the idea.

Randy could see the pensive and dumbfounded look on Daniel's face and stopped talking. The two exited the Frosty Freeze, entered Daniel's vehicle, and continued west on Interstate 10 towards Victorville. They continued driving without speaking a word.

Chapter Six

Eduardo

While he sat down at the desk that he shared in the office at the rear of the store, Eduardo Flores began speaking in a fast and high voice which he often used when he was excited. When he was excited, it became more apparent that Eduardo spoke in a Dominican accent, but no one knew that he had not grown up there. He continued patronizing Sam about how he could be a great salesman if Sam only focused on getting his work done rather than socializing with the other employees. Eduardo was especially concerned about the female customers who often complained about Sam's wandering hands. Sam was warned that if complaints continued to come in, Eduardo would have no choice but to terminate Sam for harassment. Eduardo reminded Sam that he was a married man and that he needed to honor his marriage as well as obey the company's anti-harassment policy. Sam listened attentively because he knew that Eduardo would have to put a disciplinary memo in his personnel file.

Eduardo was just the assistant manager of RadioShack at the store in Montclair. After working there for nearly six months, Eduardo believed that he should be promoted to the store manager and that he could even manage a couple of stores for the company someday. He wanted to share his goals with Sam and encourage Sam to have his own goals, but something told him not to. Sam, like many of the associates under Eduardo's supervision, repeatedly challenged Eduardo's management style. The sales associates often complained to their store manager and even to the district manager that Eduardo was overbearing, believed everyone should never question him even if he was blatantly wrong or mistaken, and believed that he knew better how to run the store compared to the store manager who had worked for RadioShack for over twenty years.

Eduardo had received his second write-up already for his own violations of company policy. He knew that Sam was aware of it so Eduardo decided not to push the conversation any further. Eduardo's latest write-up involved an angry challenge to the store manager Ahmed's authority. Ahmed was a devout Muslim and wanted his brother, Abdul, to enroll in the company's management training program. Eduardo believed that this nepotism was wrong especially because Abdul never even worked for RadioShack. Of course, Eduardo felt that he should be enrolled in the management training program and sternly told Ahmed that. An exchange of heated, choice words resulted after Ahmed rejected Eduardo's request. Later on that evening, Eduardo spoke to his wife, Maria, about it. He was angry because he believed that Ahmed's unwillingness to let Eduardo into the training program stemmed from Eduardo's decision not to accept Ahmed's invitation to attend the local mosque several months prior. Eduardo was very interested in attending and originally eagerly accepted the invitation. It was only after Maria learned that Eduardo was seriously considering converting to Islam that he ultimately decided not to attend. Maria's threats were enough to dissuade him. She was raised a Christian even though she was not attending church at the time. However, Maria would not allow her husband to convert. It was out of the question. Maria told Eduardo that she would not wear a hijab or perform the salat five times a day. Maria had heard that women prayed in a separate area of the mosque and she did not believe in such separation even if it was meant to allow women to better serve God in private. She told Eduardo that she did not want to live that way and that she would divorce him if he converted. Faced with such threats, he reluctantly never did.

When speaking with Maria about Ahmed's decision to allow Abdul to attend the management training program, Maria could sense Eduardo's anger towards her. Eduardo blamed Maria for Ahmed's refusal to allow Eduardo to participate in the training program. He repeatedly told her that on the night that he was written up and almost every night since. Now that Eduardo had difficulty at work because sales associates like Sam would no longer listen to him, his anger and frustration towards Maria grew. He tried to hide his anger during the meeting with Sam, but Sam knew it was boiling beneath the surface. Sam was secretly pleased, but knew better than to bring it up. Once Sam left Eduardo's office, Eduardo grabbed his cellphone and began texting Keshia. Keshia was a young, buxom black woman who also worked as a sales associate at the same RadioShack where Eduardo worked, but she primarily worked on the day shift. Eduardo met her earlier that year at the company's annual convention. Since then he tried to get her to work on the night shift. Once he used his managerial position to schedule her to work hours at night when Eduardo was also working. The other associates realized what was happening so they complained to upper management. Eduardo was only verbally reprimanded when he insisted that it was an innocent mistake. Keisha could no longer work evenings as a result. Eduardo could not speak with her in person while working. So he tried other means to communicate with Keisha.

"It's another long day. Sam's acting up again," was the contents of the text message that Eduardo sent Keshia.

Eduardo's cellphone indicated that the text message was delivered and shortly thereafter indicated that it was read by the recipient. Ellipses indicated that Keshia was typing her response. Eduardo eagerly awaited it. He needed Keshia's support and understanding. In Eduardo's mind, Keshia was different from Maria. Keshia was supportive and encouraging and submissive the way Eduardo preferred. Eduardo originally married Maria because she was independent and spoke her mind. Eventually, Eduardo considered those characteristics as being argumentative and unsupportive.

Eduardo's cellphone received Keshia's text: "You can do it, sweetie. You're an excellent manager and the company will come to realize that. Soon they will know they made a mistake."

Upon reading the text, Eduardo smiled and the heaviness of his heart lightened. "Thanks, honey. You are so supportive. I don't know what I would do without you," he typed.

"Are you coming over tonight?"

"Sorry, I can't. I have to work late," he responded.

Eduardo knew that the real reason that he could not have a late night tryst with Keshia was that his brother-in-law, Daniel, was coming into town to plan Michael's funeral. Eduardo regretted that and wanted to spend time with Keshia instead. He knew that Maria would be expecting Eduardo to play the good host to her brother. Any attempt by Eduardo to avoid coming home would only upset Maria and would make things worse. Maria already suspected that Eduardo was being unfaithful. She received a text meant for Keshia the prior month. When Maria confronted him about the text, Eduardo pretended that he really intended to send the text to Maria, but the flowery, romantic language was atypical of how Eduardo would text his wife. Afterwards, Maria kept a close eye on Eduardo's cellphone. She knew his passcode and would check the cellphone at night for texts when he was asleep. He suspected her of doing that because she had done it the year before when Eduardo was having an affair with LaWanda. Eduardo learned to delete his texts while at work before going home so that Maria could not find them. He was often afraid that he would forget to delete them at night. He was more afraid that Maria would log online into the Sprint website where she could actually see the texts exchanged with Keshia and the other women that he often texted and called on a regular basis. Although Eduardo was tech savvy, he knew that he could not do anything about deleting the texts or the phone numbers in the cloud. He only hoped Maria would not figure it out herself.

"I'll miss you, my Oso." It was Keshia's nickname for Eduardo. She did not speak Spanish, but knew a word or two.

"I'll miss you too, sweetie." Eduardo said including a heart emoji to emphasize his passion. "*She'll like that*," he thought.

Eduardo decided to text LaWanda: "What's happening in your world? Miss you." No response was forthcoming. "*She'll make me wait a day or two before responding. But she will*," Eduardo thought. That thought made him smile.

Eduardo then texted Maria: "What time is Danny coming over?" He tried not to let his frustration come across in his text.

"He should be here around five. Randy is coming with him."

After receiving the text from Maria about Randy, Eduardo knew that he had to come home. He was even more disappointed.

"I have to work late," he typed. "But I'll be there."

"You better. I'm counting on you."

Since Michael's death, Eduardo came home early every night and spent more time with Maria rather than working late like he would normally do. She would talk about her memories of Michael as a child. Once in a while, Eduardo would hug Maria when she would tear up while talking. He would assure her that everything would be okay. However, Eduardo never liked Michael because of Michael's abusive attitude. When Maria set the rule that no kids thirteen years old or younger could attend their wedding, Eduardo did not care that Michael could not attend. Surprisingly, Eduardo was very protective of Marie even though she was not his actual daughter. He knew Maria loved her only daughter very much. Eduardo wanted to keep his relationship with Marie on a level that would make his wife happy. Eduardo would not forgive Michael for pushing Marie during the Thanksgiving dinner at Lucia's house, even if Maria had asked him to. But she never did. Eduardo was content that he no longer had to deal with Lucia and Michael after they moved to Georgia. He now resented having to be involved in the funeral and especially having to contribute financially. More importantly, Eduardo resented the time that he now had to spend away from Keshia. But he knew that coming home early each night would lessen Maria's suspicion. So he tolerated the temporary inconvenience.

Eduardo was not looking forward to going home that evening. He really did not need to work late, but he knew that this was the only excuse Maria would accept. Making money as the man of the house was important to her. She would tolerate his late nights at work because of it. Eduardo was responsible for the scheduling as the assistant store manager, but he would schedule himself to work on Friday and Saturday evenings and even on holidays. Maria was often alone then and frequently complained to Eduardo to revise the schedule so that he could be home on the weekends and holidays, but he refused. Eduardo rationalized it as ensuring that he was there during the busiest times of the week so that the company would see his great managerial skills and consider him an essential employee. Unfortunately, his temper always seemed to get the best of him and would undermine his efforts to prove his value to the various companies that he worked for. Eduardo lost each of the five jobs that he had while married to Maria as a result of his temper. He was often unemployed for long periods of time. Almost two years passed before he got the job at RadioShack and now he was on the brink of losing that job as well. Eduardo thought that staying late and working hard would show upper management that he was committed and would forestall the inevitable. He tried to convince himself of this, but his nagging doubt was difficult to cast aside.

Eduardo continued to prepare his paperwork for that evening. The annual inventory was scheduled to occur shortly before the Christmas holiday season, requiring all of the employees to manually count each item in the store. This required all of the employees to stay late well into the evening. Sometimes employees did not leave the store until six o'clock in the morning because it took that long to count ever item. To avoid this possibility for the upcoming inventory, Eduardo came up with a plan to heavily discount a lot of the merchandise so that it would be sold in advance of the annual inventory. That way the employees, including Eduardo, could leave earlier. He spent the entire evening drafting the proposal and estimating the amount of profit that could be made as a result of various proposed sales. Eduardo also knew that he could earn significant monies in spiffs (bonuses) if the sales were successful. That would allow Eduardo to pay for additional dates with Keshia without Maria being the wiser. He could simply lie that HR screwed up his paycheck and did not pay him what he was entitled to and that the company would make it up to him on the following paycheck. By the time the next payday rolled around, Maria would have forgotten about the discrepancy in his bonuses. Eduardo could spend the extra money any way that he wanted without Maria's knowledge or control.

Before leaving work that evening around eleven p.m., Eduardo texted Keshia one last time: "Miss you, sweetie. Wish I was in your arms." He quickly deleted the text and her response, locked the store, got into his car, and drove home. When Eduardo got home around midnight, Randy and Daniel were asleep in the guest bedrooms. Maria was in bed half asleep and was waiting for him. He gave her an obligatory kiss on the forehead and began changing into his pajamas.

"How was work?"

"It was a long day. Go back to sleep. I'm just going to play some video games and will be in bed in a minute."

Maria knew that Eduardo would be up for several hours playing video games. She had to wake up early the next morning to stock merchandise at one of her stores in Hemet by eight a.m. So she did not bother to stay up any longer and went back to bed. Maria could not understand why Eduardo, a thirty-five year old man, would still play video games. She thought that he would outgrow it by now. Each year, he attended the Electronic Entertainment Expo and used his sparse vacation days to attend each day of the expo. That meant Eduardo did not have the vacation days to travel to Santa Barbara or San Diego or San Francisco for a romantic getaway like Maria desired. Eduardo spent most of his money every three or four months buying the latest, big screen television. Every year, he would purchase all of the latest video game systems from Nintendo, Sony, and Microsoft. He wanted to be the first on his block to have the newest technology. That meant that he paid full price for each television set and video game system. On top of that, he would buy every new video game on the first day it came out. He spent nearly all of his disposable income on electronics. Oftentimes, he spent more than he made and charged it. The credit card companies constantly called regarding missed payments. The late fees piled up. Over the years, two of Maria's cars were repossessed because Eduardo refused to pay the car note and would instead spend thousands of dollars on the latest television sets. Maria spent endless amounts of time trying to juggle the payments for Eduardo's nineteen credit cards, to no avail. As soon as she paid one off, the next month, Eduardo would charge that same credit card up to its limit. They were constantly in debt. Maria was unaware that Eduardo had not paid the mortgage for over six months. He was using the money to purchase lavish gifts and dinners for Keshia and sometimes other women that he would meet online or at work. Eduardo knew that Maria would fret and become upset if she learned about the lack of mortgage payments. So he never mentioned it to her.

He would simply play World of Warcraft with his friends online and ignore any of Maria's request. Because of his connections at E3, Eduardo had an advance copy of the second expansion set of the game, Wrath of the Lich King. It was suppose to come out several months later in November. Eduardo's friends were envious that he had an advance copy. He intended to play it that night regardless if his brother-in-law was there. He had been waiting for the advance copy for weeks. By the time Eduardo went to bed it was five a.m. Maria left for Hemet an hour later. Randy and Daniel woke up at eight o'clock.

"Good morning Randy," Daniel said as he woke up. "I guess I better call Sylvia to see what is happening with Michael's funeral arrangements."

The two walked downstairs and sat at the dining room table. Randy checked his messages on his iPhone while Daniel made the call to his sister in Georgia.

"Sylvia, it's me, Daniel."

"I know who it is. I have caller id, dude."

"How's mom?"

"She's been very anxious. Luckily, her church friends have been coming over to pray with her. They bring food and take turns spending time with her so that she isn't alone by herself in that house."

"I can imagine. She is taking it very hard because she found Michael."

"She's having nightmares. But her pastor laid hands on her and she is feeling better."

As they continued talking, Randy's cellphone suddenly blared out "Who Let the Dogs Out?" by the Baha Men. Sebastian and Trisha, Maria's American cocker spaniels, rushed into the dining room from the family room where they slept that night and began furiously barking at Randy's phone. The two dogs barked even louder when the digital dogs started barking as part of the song playing on Randy's phone. Randy fumbled to turn off the phone, but he dropped it instead. The ringtone continued to play while Sebastian and Trisha continued barking.

"Hold on, Sylvia. Randy, can you shut that off?"

"I'm trying."

Randy finally sent the phone call directly to voicemail and the song stopped playing.

"What was that?"

"It's a ringtone," Randy answered.

"A ringtone? Whose ringtone did you set that song for?"

"Denise."

"You set 'Who Let the Dogs Out?' as the ringtone for your wife!! Why would you do that?" Daniel was slightly frustrated by the choice and felt it was immature.

"She has been getting on my nerves lately, asking me about my affair with Minnie. I'm tired of it. I haven't seen Minnie in years, but Denise won't let it go. She keeps saying that if I want an older woman then I should get one and leave her alone. She also keeps asking if it's true that I got Minnie pregnant."

"Did you?"

The song continued again when Denise called back. Sebastian and Trisha started barking again.

"Answer the phone!!"

"I don't want to talk to Denise."

"Answer the phone so that the dogs stop barking."

Randy again tried to stop his iPhone from ringing, but Denise's call went directly to voicemail again.

"She will just keep calling and calling me."

"Doesn't she know you are with me in California to attend the funeral?"

"I never told her."

Daniel tried to ignore the disturbances and tried to continue the conversation with his youngest sister, Sylvia.

"So what is mom going to do?" he asked.

"She's planning on having a memorial service at her church on Wednesday and then they can fly Michael out to California that day or the next day," Sylvia responded.

As Sylvia continued speaking, Randy's phone rang a third time. The dogs started barking again, but this time they were in the family room which was immediately below the master bedroom. As the dogs barked, Daniel could hear a disturbance upstairs.

"Shut that off Randy."

The door to the master bedroom opened and Eduardo stumbled out. "Who the f$&# is making my dogs bark?" Eduardo yelled as he tied his white robe closed and began to walk towards the landing at the top of the stairs.

"It's Randy's phone. They keep barking at it when it rings."

"Stop that s$&@!! I'm trying to sleep. Why are you guys up so early?"

"I'm calling Sylvia about the funeral arrangements."

"I haven't gotten any sleep because of you fools."

"If you didn't play video games all night, then you wouldn't be tired. It's already 10 a.m." Daniel was surprised that he had vocalized his thoughts.

"What did you say?" Eduardo proceeded to walk down the stairs, strutting like a rooster trying to assert his dominance.

"I said that if you weren't playing video games all night that you wouldn't be so tired. I'm not goofing off. I'm calling my sister to arrange Michael's funeral."

Eduardo walked to the second to the last step of the stairwell because he was only five feet tall and Daniel was five feet ten inches tall. Eduardo wanted the extra height garnered by the steps so that he could feel as tall as Daniel. It was also another way that Eduardo intended to assert dominance. He then pushed Daniel and said "I don't give a damn about the funeral. You don't tell me what do to in my house. I will kick your a$&."

Daniel was stunned by the total lack of concern for the death of his younger brother and the attempt at dominance by his brother-in-law. Because Daniel was proud himself and would not let such an assault pass, he told Eduardo, "Try it!! Don't think I'm scared of you."

Daniel could feel the sum of all of his rage and hate welling inside of him. It's source was not just that of the immense slight by Eduardo, but also based upon his own anger over the passing of his brother, the failure of his mother to prevent it, and his tremendous guilt and self-loathing. Daniel was dejected because of the haunting dream that forewarned him of an impending death which he never considered would be Michael because, in Daniel's mind, Michael was not a true brother. Daniel was ready to pummel Eduardo the way cannons from colonial Spanish galleons could destroy an impenetrable fortress. Eduardo was unaware of this inner turmoil, but sensed something was awry.

Randy rose from the table and hurriedly walked between Daniel and Eduardo to stop them from fighting. "Guys. It's not a big deal. Don't fight. Maria will be upset."

Eduardo took a step backwards up the stairs and said "Pfft. Get the f$&@ out of my house."

"I will," Daniel said.

He knew as an attorney that getting involved in a fight and having the police come to Maria's house could negatively affect his career. In his mind, Eduardo was not worth risking his legal career. So Daniel packed his things and told Randy to do the same so that they could leave. They drove away from the house when Daniel's cellphone rang. It was Maria. Daniel figured that Eduardo had called her to get ahead of the issue and feign innocence and falsely asset that Daniel was the instigator. Daniel knew of Eduardo's past and his aggressiveness towards both Maria and her daughter, Marie. He had also seen Eduardo's fury himself and knew that Eduardo could lose his temper easily and get into a fistfight for no reason. Daniel expected Maria to rationalize Eduardo's behavior like she had done many times in the past so he refused to take her call and sent her to voicemail.

"Where are we going to stay now?" Randy asked.

"I don't know."

They continued driving until they reached the freeway and drove south on Interstate 15 towards Riverside.

"Hey, Danny. Why don't we go to the commissary at March Air Force base. I need dress shoes for the funeral and I can get a better price at the commissary."

The heaviness and anxiety from the incident with Eduardo began to wane. Daniel knew that he needed additional time to relax and to forget about Eduardo's threats and actions. Going to the base would relax him so Daniel agreed.

"We can go get some breakfast there too. I can tell them you're my guest," Randy added.

Daniel continued driving until he reached California State Route 60 and headed east towards Moreno Valley until he reached Interstate 215. March Air Force Base was realigned in 1996 and became an Air Reserve base. Randy was familiar with the base because he had served there with the 4th Combat Camera Squadron documenting combat, humanitarian, expeditionary, and training missions with still photography and video. The squadron had been based at March. Randy introduced Daniel to several of his former squadron members, including Rico and Desi. Both of them now lived in Arizona and were now stationed at Luke Air Force Base not too far from

Daniel's home in Glendale. After that, they ate at the officer's club. The two avoided discussing the incident with Eduardo and their conversation during breakfast primarily focused on Randy's desire to purchase some dress shoes for the funeral and all of the benefits he received because he served in the Air Force reserves. Daniel listened haphazardly and tried to appear to focus on what Randy was saying as he continued to nibble on his ham and cheese omelet. Randy could tell that Daniel's attention waned at times, but he continued talking as if it did not matter. Daniel's cell phone rang. This time it was his niece, Marie.

"Hey, Uncle Danny. I heard about what happened with Eduardo. He is such a jerk. I tell my mom that she should leave him, but she never does. She always takes his side…"

Marie continued talking in the hopes that she could get her uncle to open up and tell her what really happened. After awhile, while Daniel began telling her, she stopped him and told him that they could sleep at her house in Corona if they wanted to and that he could tell her the rest of the story in person. When Daniel asked Randy whether it was okay with him, Randy readily agreed.

"That will work for us, Marie. Is it okay if Randy comes too?" Daniel was uncertain whether Marie knew that Randy was with him at the time and he did not want to show up at Marie's house with Randy without previous permission.

"Sure, Uncle Danny. But don't come too soon. I have to clean the house." She laughed. She would often claim that she needed to clean the house before guests arrived, especially her uncle. But truth be told, the large house was typically cleaned and ready for guests any day of the week. Marie simply wanted it to be spotless so no one could complain, especially her grandmother, Lucia.

"Randy and I are still eating breakfast and still need to go shopping for shoes. We will leave in about two hours,"

"That's perfect. Bye Uncle Danny. I love you."

"I love you too, Marie."

Marie got off the phone with her uncle and proceeded to clean her house.

Chapter Seven

Marie

First, Marie Diaz-Anderson started cleaning the Moroccan walnut hardwood floors that led from the foyer to the family room and then into the living room with its swiveling sixty-five inch Sony LED television that was mounted over the living room fireplace. The wood flooring continued into the oversized kitchen as if it was enveloping the large kitchen island with its stainless steel double-sink and a smaller, vegetable sink bordering the east side of the island. The vegetable sink was mainly used by Marie's husband, Carlton, when he would occasionally cook alongside Marie. Carlton would mostly cook during the select holidays that they both separately celebrated with their respective families.

Marie would also have to clean the walnut wood flooring that covered the steep steps leading to the second floor of their 3,500 square-foot home that they purchased in Corona several years earlier. The home was purchased only after Marie begged Carlton to sell his two-bedroom high-rise condominium near Seal Beach. Carlton purchased before the small condominium before they met and ultimately married. She considered the condominium a bachelor pad even though she'd spent thousands of dollars redecorating the place with a woman's touch once they were married. Marie was happier living in a real home in Corona even though it was not near the beach. It was a far cry from where she was born on Chambers Lane. Marie could barely remember Chambers Lane because she left there at the tender age of four years old.

She spent nearly two years renovating their house in Corona and was very pleased at how she turned a downtrodden, foreclosed home into her personal palace. Having guests over was a great reward so she always eagerly cleaned the home to gain their tacit approval. She continued cleaning the wood flooring. The flooring continued from the steps into the master bedroom and into the hallway and then into all of the secondary bedrooms except the room above the double garage that was converted into a workout room. The floor of the workout room had light brown interlocking foam tiles that would absorb shocks when the couple exercised. They rarely used the workout room because Carlton preferred exercising at a local gym rather than at home. The foam tiles were also easier for Marie to clean, so she readily accepted the contractor's recommendation to install the tiles. Marie cleaned all of the wood flooring both upstairs and downstairs, but she did not clean the foam tiling in the workout room. Marie did not believe that the workout room would be used that weekend now that her uncle was visiting. In fact, Carlton had left for the gym once he overheard Marie inviting her uncle to stay with them. Marie anticipated that he would be gone longer than his two-hour, work-out routine. She was keenly aware how Carlton hated when guests spent the night and he would avoid coming home. Guests disrupted his routine. Carlton's OCD-like tendencies were exacerbated when anything disturbed his routine. Before leaving, Marie strictly admonished Carlton to behave once he came home because the family was dealing with her youngest uncle's death. She wanted everything to go smoother than what happened at her mother's house earlier that morning. Although Marie resented that Carlton would get out of cleaning the house with her, she knew it was for the best. He would often get in the way and insist that certain areas be cleaned in the manner and in the order that he preferred. Carlton's method of cleaning always took a lot longer than what Marie wanted to spend cleaning. She did not have the time for such shenanigans or rituals today.

The second cleaning task that Marie normally performed involved dusting her vast collection of Barbie dolls, including rare dolls like the Winter Wonderland Barbie and the Queen of the Prom Barbie. They were collector's editions valued in excess of a thousand dollars each, but Marie never intended on ever selling them unless she absolutely had to.

Her favorites were the Empress Bride and the Goddess of the Sun Barbies whose fancy outfits gave them an air of elegance that Marie frequently cherished. The dolls were stored in custom-made cabinets along the hallways of the second floor and were lit at night with SoLux museum-style lighting. Carlton originally objected to their expense, but Marie insisted that her collection deserved the best lighting. He ultimately relented. After all of the cabinets were installed and the Barbies set in place, Carlton was pleased. Marie knew that there was not enough time to follow her normal cleaning routine because her uncle and Randy would soon be leaving for her house and would likely arrive in about an hour. So she decided to skip dusting her collection of Barbie dolls. Instead, she decided to focus on the important things that would make the home look presentable once her guests arrived. This included cleaning the bathrooms, washing the linens of the beds that her guests would sleep on, and laundering the towels that they would use.

As Marie went from room to room cleaning, her sabled Pomeranian, Chloe, frantically limped behind. Chloe would follow Marie everywhere she went even though Chloe had a birth defect in her front right leg that made it difficult for her to walk. The rest of Marie's dogs lazily laid on her leather couches in the living room. They would occasionally look up when Marie walked downstairs to throw something in the trash or when she would get cleaning supplies from the downstairs closet off of the kitchen. The dogs were accustomed to her routine and learned to avoid her during those times. Her black and white Shih Tzu, Bebe, eventually exited the doggie door in the living room so that she could play in the side yard. Bebe's ears were very sensitive to sound. She left in order to avoid the slight whirling sound of the Dyson vacuum that Marie used to clean the walnut flooring. The other two dogs, Coco and Harlow, stayed inside. Both of Marie's hairless Sphynxes were laying on separate video electronic equipment for warmth. The cats typically ignored any commotion until they knew that they could again get affection from their owners. Only then would both Sphynxes scurry out for attention. Until then, they stayed aloof, rarely moving.

When Marie started cleaning the upstairs guest bathroom, she lifted the half-full garbage bag from the small stainless steel waste basket and tied the top end into a simple overhand knot. She replaced the bag with a newer one and then scrubbed the toilet and also the bathroom sink. She placed some additional toilet paper in the cylindrical storage container behind the water closet and then quickly swept the ivory marble tiles for any subtle debris. She then opened the medicine cabinet to ensure that nothing untoward was present. To her chagrin, a bottle of Prozac was inside. She had forgotten that she had hidden it there so that Carlton could not find it. A bottle of Ambien was next to it. She picked up both bottles and closed the medicine cabinet.

Marie suddenly remembered that she began taking Prozac shortly after she married Carlton. Carlton was thirteen years her senior; a gangly fellow who no one would say ranked high in the looks department. They met one day when Marie was sixteen years old and she was visiting her mother at work. Carlton was a co-worker and fancied Marie even though he was almost thirty years old. Carlton tried to befriend Marie by lavishing her with gifts. Carlton knew that Marie had a boyfriend who was her own age and who attended her same high school. He did not care. Over the years, Carlton continued trying to court Marie, especially after she turned eighteen and no longer lived at her mother's house. Eventually, she caved in despite never really falling in love with Carlton. She valued the financial security that he offered over the immature, instability of the younger men her own age. So after about ten years or more, she eventually agreed to marry him. They had a storybook wedding at the Grand Californian Hotel at Disneyland several months after their short engagement.

During their honeymoon, they stayed at the St. Regis Bora Bora Resort in French Polynesia. Their over-water premier villa had its own private pontoon overlooking the lagoon with Mount Otemanu, one of two peaks of an extinct volcano, rising in the distance. In the azure and emerald palette of the lagoon near the manmade Motu Marfo, the couple would snorkel each morning, then relax in the outdoor whirlpool of their villa, or sleep in the outdoor daybed. Dinner was eaten at one of the three resort restaurants. If the schedule varied in any way, then Carlton would experience extreme distress that would result in angry outbursts or other mood swings that were difficult to allay. His occasional outbursts only made Marie stressed and pushed her away. She tried to be understanding, but his outbursts aggravated her own emotional issues. When they came back from their honeymoon, she became depressed. The man that she thought that she was marrying was different from whom he really was. She struggled with feelings of helplessness and hopelessness coupled with regret. Carlton's OCD-like behavior upset her and caused her to yell at him to stop and fueled even more outbursts, causing an endless cycle. On occasion, she would even throw things at him out of anger. The guilt of her response was so tremendous that when Carlton threatened to divorce her unless she sought counseling, Mary willingly complied.

She visited a therapist originally two to three times a week in nearby Riverside until the sessions dwindled to once a week and then once a month. Although she begged Carlton to come with her, he never did. As a result of her sessions, the therapist prescribed Prozac for her depression and Ambien for her insomnia. The medication made Marie more docile and agreeable to Carlton's suggestions. If Carlton wanted to stay out late with his friends despite making plans to spend the evening with Marie, Marie would simply say "Okay" and let Carlton do whatever he wanted. If Carlton wanted to spend money frivolously, she would readily agree. When he decided to purchase an expensive Mercedes coupe, she had no words to the contrary. This new sense of freedom from any opposition from Marie made Carlton vehemently encourage her to regimentally take her Prozac so that any arguments could be avoided. Unbeknownst to Marie, she was like a walking corpse with little self-desire and expression. Her mind was clouded with a false sense of contentment with no basis in fact or reality. But hidden beneath her eyes was an inescapable disdain and resentment whenever she looked at Carlton.

When Marie learned of Michael's passing after her mother called her earlier in the week, Marie had become so numbed from taking Prozac that she was unable to grieve his death. There were no tears, no aching sorrow, nor even a full grasp of understanding that her uncle Michael was gone. Instead, her thoughts wandered to memories of her younger uncle. Despite the anger she once felt when Michael pushed her at her grandmother's house on Thanksgiving Day several years earlier, Marie missed her uncle. She remembered the many times she took Michael to lunch or to the movies before he moved to Georgia. He was still a child then and she was an adult. So even though he was her uncle, he had to obey her when they were out alone together. The dynamic made it easier for her to enjoy their time together. She would also frequently take him to Disneyland. She eventually purchased a season pass for him, but kept it at her house. She knew that her grandmother would never take him to Disneyland so there was no reason for a child to keep the season pass, which he could easily lose. He was always excited when Marie took him to Disneyland. Although boisterous initially, he would become silent and mesmerized when watching the gadgetry and mechanical robots and sounds of the Star Tours ride, which was his favorite ride. Once he rode it, then he calmed down; making the rest of the trip more enjoyable. The mental picture of a younger Michael smiling at Disneyland brought a smile to Marie's own face - the first one in nearly a year.

She even remembered the time when she was ten years old and Michael was two. Her uncle Daniel took them sailing in the harbor at Marina Del Rey. She could still feel the salty air breezing through her hair and could hear the screaming of the seagulls as they sailed closer to the open waters of the Pacific. The seagulls appeared to encircle them from above. She even remembered naming one of the seagulls Jonathan after a fable by Richard Bach that her uncle Daniel once read to her. Michael was exhilarated and would speak of the trip often.

Those were the happy memories that now filled her mind and awakened the dormant spirit of independence and tenacity that had been lost those past few years. Those past few years were clouded by her ritual consumption of Prozac. Marie no longer wanted to feel empty and no longer wanted to be like a shell of herself. The Prozac made her feel as if she were sleep-walking all day. She wanted to feel happiness again. She also wanted to feel the grief of losing her uncle Michael, even though such sadness is not always welcomed by those who have lost a loved one. She could not be free from her lack of emotions by following the status quo. So she decided to no longer take Prozac. She tossed the pills into the toilet bowl and flushed it. She also put the prescription bottle in the garbage bag in her hand and hid it in her neighbor's recycle bin so that her husband would not find it. She knew that, if Carlton learned of her decision that day, then he would selfishly try to pressure her into taking the pills again. She agreed not to relent in her resolve. A part of her fantasized about spiking her husband's drinks with dissolved Prozac so that he would obtain some relief from his OCD-like symptoms that he refused to treat despite his insistence that Marie treat her own issues. She knew that any such plans would run the risk that he would find out and could secretly do the same to her. So she resisted that temptation and insisted to herself that flushing the pills down the toilet was the right decision. A new-found sense of relief engulfed her. But that quickly faded.

Soon Marie remembered that she had spoken with her grandmother, Lucia, several weeks earlier and that her grandmother had mentioned during the telephone call that Michael was sad. Marie tried to pry about what was causing Michael's sadness, but her grandmother would not discuss any details and spoke circumspectly. Lucia simply asked Marie to pray for Michael. Although such evasion would have normally frustrated Marie and caused her to aggressively pursue an answer, her mental haze made it easier for her to ignore her grandmother's vague comments. Marie briefly understood that it involved a female student at Michael's school. Knowing that she would not be able to get any more out of her grandmother, Marie decided to call her uncle Michael herself and ask him about this girl, but he would not answer her calls. After repeated attempts to reach him, she gave up.

At the time, she never realized that the sadness that her uncle Michael was experiencing would ultimately lead to his tragic death. Although she regretted never speaking with her uncle, she knew there was nothing more that she could have done. Since he moved with her grandmother to Georgia, she was no longer close to Michael. Marie wished that things had turned out differently; that she would have called more, visited him in Georgia especially when she went to South Carolina the previous year, or flown him out to California like she did her cousins, Mariah and Yesenia. It was almost as if he no longer existed after the incident on Thanksgiving Day. The regret began to slowly consume her. To stave off the regret, Marie tried to focus on other feelings.

"Why did it have to be Michael," she pondered. "He was too young. Only twenty." Anger displaced the regret. It slowly grew into a fury that sought to lash out in other ways. "It should have been Uncle Junior," she angrily insisted as she realized that her hands were unconsciously clenched and her body slightly shaking. She tried to stop her racing thoughts and the newfound images that encircled her mind. She slowly breathed in and out through her mouth to quiet her storm, the way her therapist had shown her months before. When she finally unclenched her hands, the blood began to flow to them again and a sense of relief returned. She was ashamed about her sudden outburst. She never knew that she felt that way about Jose Luis or why. Her feelings about him never came up during her therapy sessions. In the ensuing months, however, as the Prozac haze eventually melted away, Marie's guilt would return periodically.

Despite her mixed emotions, she continued to clean the house. Just then, the doorbell rang so she walked downstairs towards the front of the house. It was her uncle Daniel and his friend, Randy. They were still discussing something, but Marie could not make it out when she opened the front door.

"Hey, Marie."

"Hey, Uncle Danny," she said as she stepped forward and gave her uncle a hug.

After a short pause, she heard: "It's me, Randy." He attempted to hug Marie, but she deftly stepped to the side, outstretched her arm, and shook his hand instead. She had never met Randy before and wondered why he would try to hug her. Although she felt uncomfortable, she wanted to make her guest feel at ease.

"Thanks for coming with my uncle. I'm sure that he needed someone to come with him on the long drive from Arizona. He hates it." Marie closed the door and showed the two in.

"Nice place!!" Randy exclaimed as he looked around the family room and saw the pool table, the Nintendo WII, and other games. There was also a vintage popcorn maker and a cotton candy machine. Various Disney movie posters were framed and hung on several of the walls. Marie had apparently converted the family room into a game room. "We'll have to play some time," he added.

"Sure. My uncle sucks at video games. I'll challenge you both to some WII bowling later this weekend. I'm a pro," Marie laughed at how she was not shy at displaying her prowess at video games. "Come upstairs. I'll show you your rooms. My Uncle Danny's room is to the left of the hallway. I hope you don't mind Randy, but the only other room available is my princess room. It's set up for a girl. Usually, my cousin Maleah stays in that room when she visits me. The daybed should be big enough for you."

"What happened to the guest room downstairs?" Daniel asked as they slowly ascending the stairs.

"I turned it into a doggie room. I took out the wood flooring myself and installed slate tile. You should be proud of me Uncle Danny."

"I am," he said.

When they reached the landing between floors, Daniel turned right toward the second set of stairs that led to the second floor. From there, he could see a poem hand-stenciled on the curved circular wall just above the front door and adjacent to the clerestory.

"That's new," Daniel asked.

"I hired someone to paint it. It's my favorite poem, Invitation, by Shel Silverstein."

Daniel stopped to read the poem aloud:

> If you are a dreamer, come in,
> If you are a dreamer, a wisher, a liar, ...

"What?" Daniel exclaimed angrily. "You know that your uncle Junior is a liar. You want him hanging around your house?" He stopped himself from saying anything more.

"Not really. But he used to tell me really good stories when I was a kid."

"They were just lies. He always lies. You just hadn't figured it out when you were a kid."

Randy was silent throughout this exchange. He wanted to say, "That's Junior alright." But felt it was out of place especially as a guest.

Daniel continued walking up the stairs with thoughts of his brother, Jose Luis, in the dilapidated motel room. Daniel still wondered if his older brother would attend the funeral or the wake. He tried to shake that thought when he entered the guest bedroom where he would be staying.

"Thanks, Marie," he said. I really do appreciate what you and Carlton are doing and letting us stay with you. It was a horrid experience at your mom's house."

Randy and Daniel eventually unpacked their luggage and relaxed in Marie's living room watching television. Once they sat down, the younger Sphynx, Tara, arose from the warmth of the video equipment and sat on Daniel's lap; purring and rubbing her cheek against Daniel's stomach to entice him to pet her. He did. The other Sphynx, Sookie, lifted her head off of the video equipment, looking in the general direction of the couch where the three humans were sitting, and then laid her head back down. She did not want to be bothered getting to know these new guests.

While watching television, Marie wanted to know every detail of what occurred at her mother's house that morning with Eduardo and his threats of physical violence. They took turns describing what happened with Randy even playing the ringtone assigned to his wife, Denise. Marie's dog ignored the sound and did not bark like Eduardo's dogs did.

"I told you they wouldn't bark," Marie proudly said.

Eventually, Marie wanted to speak to her uncle alone. So she asked him to walk outside and they sat down on the chaise lounges near the patio overlooking the lagoon pool in the backyard.

"What's on your mind, Marie?"

"I've been talking to my mom about what happens when she dies. I don't want to be alone, Uncle Danny. Once you and mom are dead, then I will be alone."

"Don't think that way, Marie. That's a long way away. By then, you will have your own kids and you won't be alone. You'll be happy. Both me and your mom will want you to be happy and move on with your life and not be sad that we have left."

"But I'm never going to have kids. So I'll be alone."

"Why do you say that? You're still young. You're only twenty-eight."

Marie proceeded to tell her uncle how her husband was infertile due to a cancer treatment that he underwent when he was in his twenties. She also had doubts as to whether she wanted kids with her husband given his OCD-like tendencies. She feared that any kids that they could have together would be burdened by that. She had a difficult time with Carlton as it was and adding children into the mix would make things unbearable for her. So she explained to Daniel that she may not have kids after all.

"Well, if things are too difficult with the two of you, perhaps it's not a good idea. But that doesn't foreclose that you may want to have children with another man if you ever decide to get married again if this marriage doesn't work out." Daniel tried to be encouraging in the face of the situation.

Marie was skeptical. She entered the marriage thinking that it would last a lifetime, but the past few years gave her concerns that it may not last much longer. She confessed that, if a divorce was in the future, then she may have difficulty trusting another man again and may choose to stay single. Daniel reassured her that it is unlikely that she would stay single for the rest of her life, which could be another fifty years or more. But this did not appear to bring her any solace.

"There's also something else, Uncle Danny."

"What is it?"

"I know you guys are having difficulty raising the money for Michael's funeral. I just don't think it's right that you guys have to contribute to the funeral. You were his brother not his father."

"This was an unexpected tragedy. No one would have thought that Michael would have died so young. So no one was prepared. You can't expect your grandmother to have a burial policy for her youngest child."

"Yeah, but I'm not worried about Michael. I'm worried about my mom. I told her that it's not fair for her to think that I should have to pay for her funeral. She's still young and she should try to prepare for the future, especially now that Michael died. She won't know how long she will live."

"Your mother can buy a burial policy or a life insurance policy. Do you want me to talk to her about that so that you don't have to worry about it?"

"I already did. She doesn't want to get one. She thinks that I should have to pay for the funeral because I'm her only daughter."

"That's not right. She has a husband. What did she say about Eduardo?"

"She knows that he's cheap and won't pay for anything. So she is looking to me and Carlton to pay for it."

"I don't think Carlton will want to pay for it. He doesn't like your mom."

"Exactly. Funerals are not cheap. My grandmother told me that it's going to cost $10,000 to $15,000 to bury Michael. Carlton is already mad that I made him contribute to Michael's funeral. He told me that he isn't going to contribute to my mom's funeral."

Daniel was upset that his mother told Marie this. He did not really blame her because he realized that she was trying to get family members to contribute. He just wished finances did not have to be an issue at this time and that they could focus on grieving and sending Michael off.

"I can't afford that, Uncle Danny," she continued. "I told my mom that if she were to die that I would cremate her. Cremation is cheap. If she's not willing to be prepared and leaves it up to me, then that's what I am going to do."

"I don't think your mom will like that."

"She doesn't. She doesn't want me to cremate her. She said, 'Don't burn me. I was already burned.' " Daniel held back his laughter, but understood that Marie was referring to his sister's car accident.

"I can't, Uncle Danny. I don't want to think about my mom dying. I don't know what I would do if she died. I really don't know what I would do if you died Uncle Danny. I would rather die first before you and my mom."

Marie began to sob. Her uncle got up from his chaise lounge, walked over to Marie, and hugged her.

Chapter Eight

Michael

On top of the worn oak dresser near the corner of the bedroom sat a digital photo frame whose eight inch LCD display flashed various pictures stored in its internal memory that Lucia Maria Sheffield treasured over her past sixty plus years. The last five she lived quietly in Marietta, Georgia. Although she cherished her recent three grandchildren from her youngest daughter, Sylvia, this was ultimately belied by the number of photos that flashed forth during the repetitive slideshow presentation. Most of the photos on the digital frame were of her youngest child, Michael. The photo that stood out the most during the idiosyncratic sequence of thirty-two pictures taken from the sixties until the present day was a photo of a young Michael, around one year old. It was a picture of Michael when he had just finished his Christening or in reality a Protestant equivalent of the Catholic sacrament honored by one of the

Charismatic churches that Lucia attended after she left the Holy Roman Catholic Church. The memory of the sacrament had faded. But sitting there atop of a grayish-blue, small mound of carpet in the photo was baby Michael. He was adorned in a pristine white suit wearing white shorts rather than pants. On his feet were white round toed Christening shoes fastened with white shoe laces and white socks that reached as high as his calves. He also wore a white bow tie. Atop his curly strawberry blond hair, which would darken as he aged, was a white hat almost reminiscent of a yarmulke. Lucia believed that Michael looked angelic. "Fresh like the driven manna" is what she told anyone who was willing to listen that day.

Also in the sequence of photos in the digital frame was a contrasting photo of Michael when he was eight years old. Michael, in fact, looked more like he was in his early teens because he was big and tall for his age. The picture of him was taken shortly after they had moved to Longmont, Colorado. It was taken in front of an oversized, seven-foot tall, rustic wood carving of an upright grizzly bear. The bear's arms and paws were at the ready as if it was going to rush pell-mell towards its prey. Michael sat on the cedar wood stump that formed the base for the grizzly bear. He wore an aqua-marine shirt with the word "Armada" emblazoned in black with long purple and gold simulated paint strokes underneath as if to highlight the word more intensely. His gleeless, slight smile betrayed him. From that point on, he rarely smiled. He would make his lips curl so as to feign happiness only for the picture's sake; but which he no longer felt. This was obvious in every subsequent photo.

Lucia could see both photos in the digital photo frame in the corner of her eye as she sat nervously on a old chair in her bedroom. She was looking towards Michael who was seated dejectedly at the foot of her bed near her. He waited patiently for her to stop talking because he did not want to interrupt his mother. He knew that interrupting her would only upset her and bring forth a wrath that she would often hide while in public or in the presence of fellow church members. Michael, however, was very familiar with her outbursts. She was sternly explaining why she could not move back to California at that time as he wished. Michael had heard it many times before and he grew tired of the excuses.

"I know mom," he angrily muttered, trying not to raise his voice and trying to still speak at a whisper's level so he would not offend her. "I just want to go home. I don't like it here."

"This is your home. We've been here for over five years now. You've gotten used to Marietta. Don't you like the boys at church?"

Michael was stunned that his mother said this. She should have known that he had not gone with her to church in well over a year. He never liked going even as a child. Now that he was twenty and had the choice to go or not, he preferred to stay home on Sundays and play video games. He felt that her last comment was grasping at any excuse not to acknowledge that he felt extremely alone in Georgia and that he disdained living there.

"Mom, you don't want to move back. Just say it. If you don't want to move back, then I will move back myself."

"How? You don't even own a car."

Michael remembered that past summer how he had taken the Greyhound bus back to California. He was supposed to meet his older sister, Maria, at the bus station because she paid for the bus ticket. Maria agreed to let him stay at her house for two weeks so that he could get away from his frustrations in Georgia. She hoped that this mini-vacation would renew their relationship and that Michael would decide to move back with his mother to California. But he never arrived at the last bus stop. Instead, at the bus stop near Perris, which was several stops before the last one in Victorville, he exited the bus and called his childhood friend, Lenard, to pick him up. Lenard drove to the bus stop and they spent the entire two weeks smoking marijuana with the rest of Michael's childhood friends from Perris. When Michael never showed at the bus stop and Maria had waited for hours, she repeatedly called him worried and wanted to know his whereabouts. But he never answered his cell phone. He let her calls go to voicemail and ignored her. Maria never phoned her mother and never told her what happened because she was afraid that doing so would worry her mother. Maria hoped that Michael would come out again the following summer and this time he would actually visit her. Telling her mother would only mean that Michael would never be given the chance to come out alone again. Michael finally returned Maria's call when he was on the return trip to Georgia and the effects of his smoking had worn off. He admitted to her what he had done and frankly told her that he would do it all over again if given the chance.

Michael knew that he did not own a car and that his mother's question about owning a car was not only rhetorical, but also sarcastic. He knew better than to ask Maria for a plane ticket home to California because of what he had done last summer, ditching her for his friends. Now that he finally realized that his mother would never move back to California, Michael contemplated calling Lenard again and having him drive to Georgia this time, pick him up, and drive Michael home. Lenard would do anything to get the ole gang back together again even if it meant driving eight days round trip. At least, that was what Michael believed.

"I'll find a way to get home," he told his mother.

"I already called Lenard's mom last year and told her what happened. So don't even think about calling him to pick you up."

Michael wondered how his mother found out. He knew Maria would never have told her. He imagined that Maria had spoken to his brother, Daniel, about what occurred because the two of them were very close and spoke daily. Michael believed that Daniel must have immediately told their mother. Daniel was a stickler for the rules and did not like it when one of the siblings, typically Jose Luis, would take advantage of any of the other siblings. Daniel knew that telling his mother about Jose Luis's shenanigans was of no avail because he was a grown adult and their mother had no desire to influence him. But Michael was still a child in their mother's eyes and he lived under her roof. Lucia believed that anything Michael did reflected on her and her Christian values so she was eager to correct Michael when he took advantage of the other siblings. In all other aspects, she had very little desire to influence Michael other than influencing his belief in God. Lucia believed that she was obligated to do as a Christian mother. Michael was disappointed that Daniel told his mother about his diversion to Lenard's house last summer. Michael knew Lenard would not drive to Georgia even if Michael asked him to. Lenard was Michael's age and also lived with his mother. Lenard's mother held similar beliefs as Michael's own mother and Michael knew that she would have sternly disciplined Lenard and that he would not dare cross his mother to help Michael again.

"Why did you do that? I hate it here!!" Michael exclaimed. "I don't want to live in Georgia. I don't want to live with you. I don't want to live at all."

"Don't say that. Please Lord Jesus cover him and protect my son."

"I hate it here. I have no friends. I have no girlfriend. Angelica hates me. Her family hates me and don't want me near her. My brothers and sisters hate me and don't want anything to do with me. There is no reason for me to live. No one will care if I am gone."

"I'll care if you are gone."

"It's like you said mom, 'It's better to be with the Lord than to be living in this sinful world alone.' At least I won't have to feel alone." Michael began to sob and he wiped the few tears from his eyes with his left sleeve. He tucked his head down almost to his lap.

Lucia rose from the chair and sat on the floor next to Michael, placed her right hand on his head, raised her left hand in the air, and began to pray. Eventually she began to speak unintelligibly. It was the angelic language that she claimed to pray in when she was filled with the Spirit. When Michael was young, he was startled and afraid when he first heard his mother speak in her angelic language. Now, he was used to it so it did not bother him. He was used to his mother praying for him and the rest of her children. This time, although he did not wholeheartedly believe in God like his mother did, her prayers for him brought a slight sense of relief. In some ways, Michael began to feel that his mother may care for him more than the church members whom she seemed to give all of her time and her priority to. He often felt slighted and ignored. His mother would give most of her attention to the numerous other individuals whom she also claimed were her "sons" and "daughters." Michael felt almost as if her real sons and daughters did not really matter to his mother.

Once Lucia finished her prayer, Michael lifted his head and told her, "I can't do this anymore. I don't want to do it anymore. Mom, can you help me?"

"What do you mean?" she inquired.

Michael proceeded to tell his mother about his suicide attempt the previous month. He had gotten a rope from one of his friends, tied it around a wooden beam on the roof of the garage, placed his neck in the noose, and pushed the chair from underneath him. Michael explained how he dangled there for a few seconds, but that his heavy weight caused the aged rope to break.

Lucia was shocked that her son had previously attempted suicide. She was completely oblivious to his attempt or the fact that he was suicidal. At first, she thought his cries for help were those of an individual just seeking attention like she had read about so many times before in various magazines. Her initial reaction was to not take Michael's threat seriously. But his last comment that he had tried it and failed made it all the more real to her. She vowed that she would not help him commit suicide because that was a sin against God. Besides, he was her son, her youngest child, and she selfishly wanted him with her even if she struggled with what God's will was at that very moment. She could not believe that it was God's will that Michael commit suicide.

"Michael, I'm here for you. I'll pray with you and I'll support you in everything that you want to do, but I'm not going to help you kill yourself."

"I know mom. I'm sorry."

Silence filled the air. But after awhile, they began to talk again. Mother and son stayed up all night talking. They talked of his childhood in Canyon Country, the brief stint living in Colorado, their house in Perris, and the tumultuous times living in Georgia just across the street from Sylvia. She even told Michael that she would move back to California and that they would even move in with his grandmother so that they could be home again. Michael was in good spirits. Lucia silently prayed to herself when Michael fell asleep the next morning. Lucia called in sick from her job that day and stayed with Michael that entire day and night. She also took off of work the second and third days as well and stayed up all night with him again. She had not slept in over forty-eight hours. On the third evening, Lucia was so exhausted that she fell asleep leaving Michael all alone that night. When she woke up, she looked around the room and did not see him lying on her bed the way she remembered him before she inadvertently fell asleep. She yelled out his name and walked down the stairs to the garage.

Chapter Nine

Sachiko

Sachiko stormed to the front yard like a sentinel on duty. His little black and white paws soared tremendously until he reached the silver, but rusting steel chain-linked fence that outlined the front of the Mendoza property. His loud yelps echoed repeatedly at the male stranger who continued to walk listlessly along the sidewalk as if Sachiko was not there. That did not matter to Sachiko. It was his solemn duty to protect the Mendoza family and he carried it out day in and day out regardless of the number of strangers passing by or the time of day. Striding back and forth the entire length of the front fence that abutted Chambers Lane, Sachiko would run and run, around the red rose bush with its prickly thorns and then straight until he reached the end of the driveway at the northwest corner of the property. His repeated rompings had etched a groove into the dirt over time and today, like every other day, his paws were soiled with the loamy, red dirt. He continued his frolic along the fence in that worn out groove as if it were guiding him towards his ultimate destination, where he had already been innumerable times before and actually needed no instruction. You could see him cautiously avoiding the rows of tomato vines that were planted along the front fence as well as the reddish-yellow Madame Jeanette chili peppers that Lucia Mendoza Sheffield loved. The chili peppers were similar to habaneros. Lucia would use them in the various meals that she prepared, even though she never cooked any Surinamese recipes.

Sachiko had been warned many times not to run inside the foot-high, white garden fence. It was installed the summer before to protect the mini-garden from Sachiko's incessant running. He could not understand why he could no longer run along the metal chain link fence anymore and why he had to circumvent the garden fence while he valiantly pursued those strangers who dared to walk by his home. But during times like these, Sachiko could not control himself. His innate urge to protect the family would overcome him. Sachiko would easily leap over the garden fence to get closer to the stranger and assert his authority. It wasn't as if it helped. The stranger was oblivious to him and maybe that is what irritated Sachiko so much such that he had to get closer to the chain-link fence to prove his point. The fence wobbled as Sachiko roared his unintelligible commands to the stranger.

"Sachiko!!! Don't run over my vegetables," Lucia screamed. You could hear her voice all along Chambers Lane, even as far away as Duncan Avenue or around the corner near Wright Road. "I tell you, Daniel. He is going to ruin my tomatoes and chili peppers again this year."

"Well, we have some more in the back garden near the nectarine tree. Those seem to grow taller and faster than the ones by the street. They also bear a bigger harvest."

"That's because Sachiko isn't stomping on them and destroying them like he does the ones in the front yard. Why does that dog do that? There isn't even a garden fence surrounding the vegetables in the back yard. He doesn't go near the vegetables there. But he has to be run every day in the garden in the front yard."

"He can't help himself. He wants to protect the family and he doesn't know any better. That's why he runs. He isn't hurting anyone."

"I'm tired of hearing him bark. Go out there and tell him to stop."

Daniel opened the rickety, screen door and slowly walked to the front yard, gazing as Sachiko. Daniel could see that Sachiko sensed him coming. Sachiko knew why Daniel was there because Daniel had done this ceremonial dance many times before with Sachiko. Today would be no different. Sachiko stopped in his tracks and tried to avoid looking in Daniel's direction. Daniel walked closer to Sachiko until he could scoop up Sachiko's little body into his arms and whisper into his ear.

"You know that you aren't supposed to run in the garden, Sachiko. You can seem to avoid the rose bush here, but you won't avoid these chili peppers or tomato plants. You know that mom is going to get mad at you if you keep ruining her tomatoes."

Daniel brought Sachiko to the southwest corner of the front yard near the granny apple tree. The apple tree was beginning to blossom. As he did every week, Daniel walked Sachiko in his arms along the route that Lucia wanted Sachiko to traverse. Daniel walked Sachiko around the rose bush, pass the garden, along the larger driveway area that was turned into a basketball court where Junior and Daniel played in front of the garage. He continued walking until he reached the double-gated fence toward the northwest corner of the property near Perry and Louise's house.

"This is where you are supposed to walk."

Sachiko growled in disagreement and sternly looked Daniel in the eyes. Daniel could feel Sachiko trying to escape his grasp, but Daniel held tighter. Sachiko relented because he knew that Daniel was his master. Even if Sachiko could escape, the ritual would repeat itself the very next day. Daniel finally let him down. Sachiko hurriedly ran back into the house, into what he deemed was the safe area where he could not get into trouble even from strangers.

Sachiko was a Lhasa Apso mixed with poodle. Daniel later learned that such dogs are called a Lhasapoo. Sachiko lacked the wooly, long hair of a normal

Lhasa. Instead, he had the curly hair of a poodle with a round, crown-like head and long-haired ears that hung down to his cheeks. Those ears lacked the typical curly hair throughout Sachiko's body. His body was sturdy with a black coat on his back and ears and face. Sachiko's underbelly was white. White hair also speckled his face, especially around his mouth and nose and on the top of his head.

The Mendoza family had Sachiko since he was a puppy. Daniel still could remember the day when his mother brought Sachiko home unexpectedly. One of her co-workers had pups and offered to give them to anyone who would take them. Later that day, Lucia Mendoza went to her co-worker's house only to find out that two pups were left. The female pup had just been given to another co-worker who had arrived ten minutes earlier. Sachiko, the runt of the litter, was the only pup left. Lucia decided to take him anyway, but she never explained why. Lucia never really liked animals. She must have brought him home for her four children. Lucia would touch Sachiko by rubbing his back with her feet. Poor dog. She never really petted him like normally people do nor played with him. Perhaps, she thought that was her children's job.

When she brought him home, all of the kids were excited, especially Maria. Because Maria was the oldest, she took Sachiko in her arms and claimed him as her own. It was Maria who named him Sachiko after a Japanese character on a television show that she loved. Never mind that the character was female and Sachiko was a male puppy. But her interest in him did not last. Maria was in her later teen years when Lucia brought Sachiko home. Maria was always out and about with her girlfriends and with any guys that she was fleetingly interested in. Because Daniel studied a lot at home, he was the main one who played with Sachiko. So Sachiko grew to know Daniel more than anyone else in the Mendoza family.

But as the years passed, like everyone else, Daniel also lost interest in Sachiko. Daniel was preoccupied with other things while in high school: the physics club, computers, watching the Bruins win at basketball, and then ultimately having to work late night and on the weekends at Montgomery Wards. Daniel never learned which family member would feed Sachiko during all those years when Daniel was busy and failed to. It must have been his mother, Lucia. Nor did Daniel remember ever seeing dog food in the house. He was certain, however, that Sachiko was feed actual dog food because his mother never believed in feeding dogs human food. Daniel's Aunt Belén would feed her dogs leftover beans and tortillas without hesitation. She never purchased any dog food.

Daniel was no longer involved with raising or training Sachiko after a few years. The daily and weekly ritual of carrying Sachiko along the front fence disappeared. Once or twice a year or so, Daniel would perform the ritual when his mother would ask. Maybe it was because Sachiko learned to avoid the front garden and the peppers and tomatoes. Maybe it was because his mom no longer minded if they were trampled upon. Although Daniel spent hours upon hours studying at home before and after work, even until the late hours of the night, Daniel no longer cared about what happened at the house.

One day, as he came home, Daniel heard a ruckus. Sachiko was under the dining room table barking and growling fiercely at his mother. She was trying to prod Sachiko out from underneath the table with a broom. Maria was there too with something else in her hand. Sachiko was snapping and chomping on the broom as he tried to avoid it. Both Lucia and Maria were yelling and screaming at Sachiko when Daniel walked in.

"What are you guys doing?"

"He tried to bite me," his mother exclaimed.

"What did you do to him?"

"Nothing. He is going crazy in his old age."

"He's not crazy and he is only a couple of years old. He just doesn't like people prodding at him with a broom." Daniel took the broom away from his mother, crawled under the table, and said, "Sachiko, come boy." Sachiko whimpered closer to Daniel as Daniel reached out for him.

"He is gonna bite you. Be careful."

"Sachiko doesn't bite."

"He tried to bite me too," Maria said.

"That's because he doesn't like you. He likes me."

Daniel reached out toward Sachiko and Sachiko crawled into his arms. Daniel brought him out from underneath the table.

"Be careful," his mother added.

Daniel walked with Sachiko in his arms into his bedroom and sat on his bed. Daniel could feel the anxiety exuding from Sachiko. Sachiko began to calm down as the noise level returned to normal in the house. Daniel slowly caressed his back.

"There, there, Sachiko. Everything is going to be alright. Did they hurt you?"

Sachiko began to fall asleep on Daniel's bed. When he had slept for a few minutes, Daniel arose and went back into the living room.

"He did try to bite me," Lucia slyly said as Daniel entered the room.

"Let me see." Daniel looked at his mother's hands and arms and could not see any scratches or bite marks. "I don't see anything."

"Listen, Daniel. He is going crazy. The same thing happened to his sister. I heard from my co-worker that she started going crazy as she got older, trying to bite everyone, and they had to put her down."

"You aren't going to put him down. He needs to be trained. I would train him but I don't have the time."

"I'm not going to pay for any training."

"Well, I'll pay for it."

"You don't have the money."

"I have some money. I just don't want to see him go. He is part of the family now and it's not right to put a dog down for nothing."

"It's not for nothing. I am afraid of him."

"I am afraid of him too," Maria said.

"Did he ever bite you?" Daniel inquired.

"No, but he growls at me, snaps at me like he is going to bite me. Something is wrong with him." Maria surprisingly sided with her mother on this rare occasion.

"He has never bitten me or tried to bite me."

In all the years prior to this, Daniel had never heard anyone in the family complain that Sachiko was mean or tried to bite them. Nor did Daniel ever see Sachiko try to bite anyone. The dog had a loving temperament and kept to himself. It was strange for Daniel to hear this from his mother and older sister now. Daniel wondered why they were saying these things. His mind fixated on that they no longer wanted anymore pets. This started after the family's second dog, Kahlani, was given away after she kept destroying everything in her sight including the slip and slide that was in the front yard. Perhaps, giving Kahlani away made it easier for the family to get rid of Sachiko because they no longer wanted to be bothered with a pet.

The Mendoza family's first pet was a British blue shorthair with a solid blue-gray coat and copper eyes. Like Sachiko, the cat had a white underbelly with white paws and white hair surrounding the tip of her nose and parts of her forehead. Her coat was dense and silky to the touch. She never really bothered with any of the kids, except to ask to be feed. Only Sylvia tried to play with her, but that was because Sylvia was young and naïve. The cat spent most of her time outdoors running the streets anyways. The family inadvertently left the cat when they moved from the house on Serrano to the house on Heliotrope because they could not find the cat on the day of the move. Weeks later, she appeared at the new house on Heliotrope, having walked 3-4 miles to get there with no knowledge of where the family had moved. The Mendoza family was surprised to see her again. She lived with the Mendoza family at Heliotrope for two months and one day she left. No one knew why. That was years ago and there was no way that she could find the Mendoza family again because they had moved twenty miles or so away to Chambers Lane. Besides, the family had forgotten all about her by the time they moved to Chambers Lane the following year.

Many months passed and Daniel had forgotten the incident with his mother and Maria trying to fend out Sachiko. His mother never mentioned getting rid of Sachiko again. Until one day, after walking home from school, Daniel did not hear Sachiko's excited bark that typically welcomed him home. Daniel looked for Sachiko, but he was not there. He ran along Chambers Lane calling out Sachiko's name. Sachiko had never gone outside the chain-linked fence before except once or twice when the double-gate leading to the garage was left opened. Daniel feared the worse this time. Perhaps, Sachiko was injured on the side of the road. Daniel frantically walked up to the corner of the street until he reached Duncan Avenue and looked both ways. He could not see any dog on the street and yelled Sachiko's name again and again. Daniel continued walking along Chambers Lane and came to Pope Avenue, then passed Virginia Avenue and continued walking until he arrived at Atlantic Avenue. The hustling bustle of this four-lane major street confused him.

"*Surely, Sachiko did not run this far away from home,*" Daniel thought.

Daniel walked back home hoping to see Sachiko there. Daniel thought that he may have missed Sachiko and that he was sleeping under Daniel's bed like he usually did. As Daniel walked back, he thought perhaps Sachiko headed in the other direction towards Wright Road, which fronted the freeway or maybe Sachiko went so far as to walk to the Los Angeles river basin. Daniel's rushing thoughts subtly encouraged him. He found himself unknowingly galloping at a faster pace and was home sooner than he expected.

By the time Daniel got home, his mother's car, a tan Ford Maverick with a dark brown, vinyl-covered top, was parked in the driveway. Maybe his mother knew where Sachiko was. Daniel walked into the house and saw his mother on the couch. She sat there as if nothing happened.

"Where is Sachiko?"

"I had to do it. You know he was going crazy."

"Where did you take him?"

"I didn't take him. Reuben did." Reuben was Daniel's closest, childhood friend at the time. He was several years older and owned a car. Reuben had gotten Daniel the job at Montgomery Wards. They drove to work together when they were scheduled at the same time. Reuben made sure that they were scheduled at the same time because he knew that Daniel had no car and that Daniel's mother would not drive him to work. Lucia said that, once she got home, she did not want to have to leave the house again. So if Daniel was scheduled to work in the evenings, he either had to walk the forty-five minutes to Montgomery Wards or Reuben would stop by the house and pick Daniel up.

"Where did Reuben take him?" Daniel asked.

"I asked Reuben to take him to the pound."

"I'm going to get him back."

"He isn't coming back."

"Why not? I want him back. They'll give him back to us. I'll call Reuben and have him take me to the pound."

"They don't have him."

"What do you mean?"

"I mean he is gone."

"Gone?"

"Yes, gone. I couldn't have him anymore in the house. He tried to bite me. He tried to bite your sister."

"That was only once."

"Once is enough. I didn't want to deal with him like that. You know he was going crazy, just like his sister went crazy."

"He wasn't crazy."

"Well, it doesn't matter. They put him down. So he is dead."

"Dead?"

"Yes."

"Why did you do that? Why did Reuben do that?"

She had no explanation. Daniel never spoke to Reuben again for the rest of his life.

Chapter Ten

Sylvia

As she sat askew on the left side of the worn, tan sofa in her family room on the second floor of her rented condominium, Sylvia hushed her kids one last time to be quiet. She wanted her children to slow their raucous playing while she readied herself for the day to come. Her long flowing black hair was speckled with gray, which started, much like her father when she was only thirty years old. Her older siblings did not have any gray hair. This embarrassed Sylvia slightly. At first, Sylvia embraced her aging features because they reminded her of her father, Marcelo Robles. Everyone else on her father's side of the family also prematurely grayed. It was apparently an Ecuadorian trait or so it seemed. Sylvia believed this because no one from the Puerto Rican side of her family grayed so early in their life. When she was in her mid-thirties, single with a child of her own and no immediate family members living in Georgia,

Sylvia Robles wanted or believed that she needed a man to take care of her. So she started the painstaking process of dying her hair black every so often. She thought that the darker, black color gave her an Amerindian look and highlighted her supposedly Incan features which stood out even more now because of her pale, round face. Gone was her darker, hued skin of her youth when she enjoyed the lazy summers in California. At times, she even wondered if her ancestry included those of the original Quitu tribe or perhaps even the Cara tribe that traversed the Esmeraldas River and conquered the Andean Valley. These thoughts were flights of fancy. Sylvia knew little of her Ecuadorian ancestry. Any bits and pieces she did know were from stories that she long ago heard as a child on those occasional visits to her father's family's house in Downey. When Sylvia would visit her uncle, Gallo, and his wife, Beatriz, and other family members, they would share stories of when they lived in Quito, Ecuador as small children. These were vague memories now. Sylvia could not always separate the truth from her imagination, which was interwoven in her subconscious. Her fanciful thoughts brought her comfort in moments like these.

Sylvia continued to slowly brush her hair until the length that lay beyond her shoulders and almost to her navel festooned into gentle waves whose subtleties betrayed a brewing storm within her. In the safety and solitude of Georgia away from her older siblings, Sylvia could avoid her childhood woes. She never asked to be treated special by their mother.

Lucia always treated Sylvia special because she was born of a union from a man that her mother deeply loved. As a child, Sylvia was too young to understand and appreciate that the kindness that she one-sidedly received and enjoyed came at a great cost to her older siblings. Little did she realize that they smiled frequently and impetuously towards her because they were forewarned to treat the much younger Sylvia with utmost care almost akin to royalty, lest they face their mother's unending wrath. That, however, did not prevent them from secretly displaying contempt. Maria would comb Sylvia's hair every morning before school; secretly hoping that any knots would make it more difficult and painful. Jose Luis would walk her to school, but take the long way there; making her late, and unsuccessfully trying to blame her when they eventually came home. He relished those moments when he would try to get Sylvia in trouble by doing various things. One time, he scribbled her name on the walls in a child-like manner with crayons so that their mother believed that Sylvia had done it. Jose Luis became dejected when the punishment Sylvia received was not nearly as severe as he had hoped. Daniel would simply argue with her and haphazardly use his intellect to confuse her when he was supposed to be helping her with her homework. Sylvia no longer had to deal with this duplicity and guile now that she lived on the east coast away from the rest of the family.

At the time, however, Sylvia was too little to realize that her own mother treated her older siblings differently because the older kids reminded Lucia of her failed, abusive marriage. She could not appreciate the difference. Sylvia had nicer clothes compared to the tattered clothes that the older children wore. Lucia had applied for and received a credit card that she exclusively used to purchase things for Sylvia. Every month Sylvia had new clothes purchased with the credit card. The other kids were only allowed two sets of clothing a year and only once school started.

Sylvia had her own kitchen cabinet above the refrigerator where Lucia would store food that only Sylvia could eat. "Sylvia's food" included better and sweeter cereal, snacks and cookies for the afternoon, and sodas and microwaveable items that the other kids could not eat. Her siblings could merely watch Sylvia eat her "food" from afar. If they were hungry, the older kids were told to eat the fruit from the many fruit trees in the yard. Their house on Chambers Lane had a granny Apple tree, a plum tree, a nectarine tree, an apricot tree, and an orange tree. In some ways, the older kids did not mind at times because the flesh of a newly plucked fruit was delicious and refreshing. But they still yearned to eat pastries and other sweets especially those Sylvia could eat. Lucia would purchase these pastries for her youngest daughter from the Dolly Madison bakery near downtown Los Angeles.

The older kids also had to do chores. They had to clean their rooms, wash the dishes, vacuum and clean the house, and fold the laundry. The boys also had to take out the trash and mow the lawn and perform other duties that were traditional assigned to males in addition to their other chores. Sylvia was not even responsible for cleaning her own bedroom. Lucia would. Sylvia did not know that her older siblings resented this.

Although Sylvia was catered to by her mother and the older children, she still felt estranged from her older siblings and somewhat of an outcast. She initially attributed the difference in how she was treated to being the youngest child. But as she grew older, she believed at times that the older siblings treated her differently because they knew that she had a different father with a different last name. Sometimes she believed that her siblings treated her differently because she did not look anything like them. The older three kids were closer in age. But all that changed when Michael was born. Sylvia was already a teenager. Now that Sylvia was no longer the youngest child, she no longer received the special treatment from her mother, who was now married to Michael's father. The older siblings had moved out of the family home because they were now adults. So Sylvia no longer could rely on them.

By the time she was fifteen, Sylvia longed for the approval of her father. She rarely saw him. He no longer requested that she spend summers with him which was allowed in the child custody agreement. He now conveniently chose to ignore that provision. Although she was his only child, Sylvia felt like her father disapproved of her. She feared that she became the child who seemed to only want her father around when she needed something. Marcelo repeatedly voiced that he never heard from his daughter unless she needed money. When she moved away to Georgia at eighteen, he appeared relieved. Marcelo thought that the distance would help Sylvia to grow up and become independent. When the calls from Georgia for money first came, he reluctantly agreed. Ultimately, he stopped and would not take her calls, especially when she was living with a man, whether that was her husband or a boyfriend. Marcelo did not believe in supporting her men. Sylvia never stopped calling if she needed anything.

When Sylvia was in her early thirties, Lucia moved to Georgia to be closer to her youngest daughter. Sylvia was pregnant with her second child, Yesenia. Ultimately, Lucia rented a house across the street from Sylvia's condominium. The close distance made it easier for Sylvia and her children to spend time with their grandmother. Lucia would babysit on occasion and even clean the condominium at times. But as always, Sylvia asked for money when she lost her job or when it was a birthday or a holiday. Sylvia did not want to spend her own money on such expenses. Sylvia would make her mother feel guilty that she was raised without a father and would take advantage of that when any opportunity arose. There was the car note that Lucia cosigned after Sylvia decided that she needed a new car, but later she would not pay the bill. This forced her mother to pay it or risk getting bad credit. Then there was the time when Sylvia owed back taxes and she asked her mother to loan her two thousand dollars. Sylvia also never repaid her mother. There were the many trips to Disney World each summer with the kids when Sylvia would ask her mother for spending money. Usually, the monies Lucia gave Sylvia ended up being the bulk of what Lucia spent during Christmas. When Christine was born and then Bernardo, Sylvia continued to ask for even more money. She refused to see how the financial strain was not only impacting her relationship with her mother, but also her relationship with her other siblings. They were aware of her constant requests even though both Sylvia and Lucia adamantly denied it.

Not only did Sylvia not get along with her older siblings, she also did not get along with Michael. When he moved to Georgia with their mother, Michael did not stop his bullying ways. Sylvia was afraid of him. She saw how often Michael cursed at their mother, slammed doors when his mother would ask him to do things around the house, spit in her face, and repeatedly shake his tightly clenched fist when he did not get his way. Michael would also curse at Sylvia, especially when she acted like the older sister and tried to protect her mother from his abuse. He would even bully Sylvia's kids, which she really resented. Michael would never pay any attention to Sylvia because he believed that everything she said or did was just her way of trying to interfere with his relationship with their mother so that Sylvia could isolate her from Michael and take advantage of her financially.

When Sylvia learned that Michael had committed suicide, she was surprised. Over the years, Sylvia told her older sister, Maria, that she believed Michael's temper along with his eccentric actions like torturing the neighbor's cat and almost setting fire to the house were similar to that of a profile for a future murderer. Maria dissuaded Sylvia from such thoughts and tried to allay her fears. But even Maria had to admit that Michael's actions correlated with a future murderer at least as far as Maria knew from various crimes shows that she watched on television over the years. The pair feared that Michael may someday murder their mother. They were loathe to tell her themselves, but they told both Jose Luis and Daniel about this fear. Both brothers were also concerned and readily agreed that they had feared for their mother's safety as well.

On that early morning, seated on her tan sofa in her condominium, Sylvia felt guilty over her secret but profound relief that Michael had passed first and that her own mother was still alive. Earlier, while her children were still asleep, Sylvia prayed for the soul of her younger brother and asked the Lord for forgiveness at the same time. Her prayers temporarily allayed her fears, but, a few hours later, now that she had to phone her brother, Daniel, in California, her guilt resurfaced.

"Hey, Daniel. You awake?"

"Of course. How could I answer my cellphone if I wasn't?" Daniel could hear Christine and Bernardo playing in the background, but trying to be quiet about it so as not to disturb their mother.

Sylvia laughed. "You're silly. Can you talk?"

"Sure." Daniel slowly walked up the stairs to the bedroom where he was sleeping in Marie's house without excusing himself with Randy and Carlton, who were watching a football game in the family room downstairs. Tara stealthily followed him a few paces behind. Daniel refused to speak again until he reached the bedroom and shut the door. This way the others could not hear the conversation. "What do you need?" At all other times, Daniel would have expected Sylvia to ask him some legal question. Typically, she would call Daniel about some credit issues that she was having or landlord-tenant law, but oftentimes it was about some criminal issues involving herself or her husband. Today was obviously different.

"Mom wanted me to let you know that she had a wake and a small memorial service today at her church."

"Really? She never mentioned that." Daniel felt uneasy that strangers across the country were participating in what he deemed a private, family affair. Sylvia could sense that in his voice.

"Her pastor thought it was a good idea because there are so many people at the church who knew Michael and who know mom and who want to be there for her. So mom agreed. I think it made her feel better too."

"Uhuh," Daniel wondered why Sylvia was telling him this.

"Well, her pastor asked for an offering during the memorial and the church members raised about two thousand dollars to pay for Michael's funeral." At all other times, Sylvia would have added "Praise God" or something to that effect, but she was keenly aware that Daniel was not in the mood to hear it, especially after his early encounter at Maria's house yesterday with her husband.

"What is she going to do with the money?" Daniel was concerned that the amount of money would tempt his mother to spend it on other things so he awaited the response. His mother was frugal, but never really had large amounts of cash before. She would often borrow money from her own mother who was in her eighties at the time. But that was only for a couple of hundred dollars here or there, depending on what Lucia wanted or needed. Her ex-husband would never help Lucia out financially so she rationalized borrowing money from her mother or her sister, Belén. The family believed that Sylvia took after her mother when Sylvia began repeatedly asking money from family members. But Lucia never saw it. Daniel was afraid that the lure of such large amounts of money was inescapable.

"For Michael's funeral, of course," Sylvia mentioned with trepidation.

Daniel was relieved. His mother had insisted that Michael be buried at the Eternal Valley Memorial Park in Canyon Country in the hills just off of Sierra

Highway. She wanted him to be buried in Canyon Country even though Michael had not lived there in nearly fifteen years. Lucia did not want Michael to be buried in Compton near her own family because Michael never lived there. Lucia also felt that the cemetery in Compton was unsightly and unkept. That decision was financially costly to the family who were already struggling with the unexpected expense along with the sudden grief. The outer burial container needed for the hilly landscape in Canyon Country and the bronze and granite memorial and base requested by Lucia together cost over three thousand dollars. Then there was the additional expenses associated with the plot and other numerous fees charged by the mortuary. The total cost was overwhelming. Daniel had used monies from his second mortgage just to pay the thousands of dollars that he contributed in order to bury his younger brother whom he barely knew and rarely saw. The collection money from his mother's church was clearly welcomed, but Daniel did not want to show it or let anyone know because he knew that the family would hold it against him even though most were unwilling to contribute to the significant cost.

"I thought you should know," Sylvia added.

"How's mom doing?" Daniel inquired in order to change the subject and divert any suspicions.

"A lot better. Her church friends have been coming over to her house and praying with her. Some even have brought over homemade dinners for her and other meals." Sylvia seemed proud and wanted her brother to know about the Christian kindness and grace that the church members displayed.

"That's nice of them. Did you know what was going on?" Daniel was hesitant to ask, but needed some answers.

"Oh, God, no. No. Mom never told me."

"Did she tell you that he tried to commit suicide before?"

"No! She didn't. I never knew he tried it before. Had I known what was going on, I would have helped out. I wouldn't have let mom stay up by herself with Michael for three nights. She's too old to do that. I would have stayed up with Michael too."

"Do you know why she never told her pastor or anyone from the church?"

"I have no idea. I know Michael hadn't gone to church in a long while. Maybe she thought he wouldn't listen to them. I don't know." Sylvia felt uneasy with this line of questioning, but she was used to it from her older brother. He had been this way as a child even before he attended law school.

"I wish she would have told me or at least Maria," Daniel sulkily responded.

"What could you have done?"

Daniel knew that he did not have that type of relationship with his younger brother. Daniel hoped that had he known that Michael felt that none of his siblings liked him, that he would have tried to reassure Michael that he was wrong or at least promise Michael that he would try harder in the future to be a part of his life. Perhaps Daniel would convince Michael that he would visit Georgia or call at times. Daniel thought that maybe if he had talked to Michael, he could have convinced Michael to reach out to Sylvia because she lived the closest. But these were only thoughts to assuage his own concerns so he did not express them to Sylvia. Both Sylvia and Daniel felt hopeless in that moment. Silence filled the air.

After a while, Sylvia broke the silence. She informed Daniel that their mother was moving back to California because she could no longer stay in the house after what happened. The memory of that place haunted Lucia and she wanted to get away from it all, not just the home itself, but all of Georgia.

"She blames me, Danny. That's not right. I had nothing to do with it!!"

"I don't understand. Why does she blame you?"

"Mom thinks that, if she never would have moved to Georgia, then Michael would have never committed suicide."

"What?!"

"Well, I am the reason that she moved to Georgia with Michael. Mom wanted to be closer to me after Yesenia was born. She sold the house in Perris and everything."

"It's not your fault, Sylvia. That was mom's choice. She didn't have to move to Georgia. She could have just visited you for a couple of weeks, but she wanted to leave everything behind and start a new life. You're not responsible for that choice."

"I know. I tell myself that. And the Lord tells me that I'm not responsible. If I were, the Holy Spirit would convict me."

"Alright."

"Mom thinks Georgia is cursed because the last time she was in Georgia grandma died. Mom blames me that she wasn't in California and could not be there to comfort her sisters or arrange grandma's funeral. She feels guilty about it and, now with Michael, she is even more upset about it."

He could sense Sylvia's exasperation. Daniel knew that there was nothing that he could say to Sylvia to alleviate the hurt that his mother caused her with such unspeakable words. Although his mother and sister both shared the same Christian beliefs, they also bought into some unbiblical Christian mysticism that he did not understand and did not now want to rebut, especially at this moment. Past efforts were futile. So he avoided doing so again.

"All I can say, Sylvia, is that it's not your fault. Not Michael. Not grandma. You don't have any responsibility for anyone's death. It's totally unfair to blame you. I don't know who is telling mom to think those things, but I wish they would stop." Daniel suspected that it was his older sister, Maria. He had heard from other family members that Maria told their mother that, if she did not move back to California, that something bad might happen, like the death of her ex-husband. Lucia was appalled by this comment, but worried nonetheless.

"Thank you, Danny. It means a lot to me. Maria has always been jealous of my close relationship with mom. She doesn't have a close relationship with mom and she is trying to ruin my relationship. Maria is jealous that mom is there for me and not her."

"Have you talked to Maria about it?"

"I tried. She won't answer my calls. They go straight to voicemail. I was so angry that I left a message telling her that she was wrong for all that. I used some choice words. I normally don't curse, but she made me so mad. God will forgive me."

"Do you want me to talk to her?"

"There's no point. It's too late. Mom canceled her return flight to Georgia after the funeral. She has made up her mind and it's all Maria's fault."

"Why don't you talk to mom about it?"

"You know mom. She won't talk to me about it. She doesn't want to get in the middle of things between me and Maria. She's always been that way. She says it's God's will and there's nothing that she can do about it except follow it."

"Uhuh."

"I don't know what I am going to do without mom. The kids are going to miss her. Maria told mom that the kids don't like being around her and claims they give her dirty looks. But that's not true. You know mom. She is difficult. But the kids really enjoy her. They are already asking about when she is coming back, but I don't have the heart to tell them yet. I'm also going to miss her. Mom always loved going with me to my job and helping me clean up the offices with me."

"Did you pay her?"

"Danny, you know mom did that because she wanted to help me out. Maria told mom that I am using her and that she is too old to do that. But mom really loves doing it. I'm not going to turn down her help just because Maria doesn't want mom to do it. Who is she? She is always trying to tell people what to do just because she is the oldest. I'm a grown woman. I don't need anyone telling me what to do. Mom doesn't either."

"Sounds like there is nothing that you can do. I talked to mom about it already and she is very upset about it. She doesn't want to deal with all of this right now. She said that she called Southwest and they were willing to work with her. But it's too late to get the flight special again because it ended. I don't thinks she will ever move back, but she may come out and visit after awhile. Just give it time. She doesn't want to remember what happened with Michael. Maybe in a year or two. You can always come visit her with the kids in California."

"I don't like California. There's too much drama there. I wish you guys would move to Georgia. They pay you better. The housing costs are cheaper."

"You know I don't like the South."

Daniel did not want to get into this again now. Sylvia had been trying to get her family to move back to Georgia for nearly two decades. Almost everyone in the family moved there except Maria and Daniel.

They would never do so. Now Lucia and Jose Luis were back in California and Michael would be buried there. Sylvia would be alone again in Georgia except for her own kids. She was going to have to accept it and she knew it.

Chapter Eleven

The Funeral

Early that morning just after dawn and before her husband woke up after another one of his long nights playing video games, Maria walked downstairs, poured herself some coffee, and then sat once more at her dining room table which overlooked her backyard. She slowly sipped her coffee, gripping the bottom of the ceramic mug tightly with her right hand and holding the handle with her left. She looked into the mug while sipping; noticing the gentle wafts of steam which revealed the intensity of the fluid and enjoying the aroma of Arabica beans filling her nostrils as well as the ambient air. She dreaded that Michael's funeral was later that afternoon, but she decided to finally call her younger brother, Daniel, to discuss the funeral arrangements. She was now able to discuss it without getting overly emotional and without feeling guilty like she had when she first learned of it. This morning was an opportune time to speak to Daniel since what happened with her husband, Eduardo. Eduardo was fast asleep. He could not overhear the conversation or in any other way interfere. She had let the dogs out to avoid a similar commotion.

"Hey, Danny." She had expected him not to answer and to avoid her at the funeral.

"Hey, Maria. Is there anything that you want?"

"I just heard."

"What did you hear?"

"I heard that cousin Stephan is going to give Michael's eulogy."

"Who told you that?"

"Well, I know that mom originally asked you to give the eulogy because you are a lawyer and can speak eloquently in front of everyone. But she spoke to Aunt Isabel earlier this week and Isabel said that only a pastor should give the eulogy. So mom decided that Stephan should do it because he is an ordained minister at his church."

"I've never heard that only an ordained minister can give a eulogy. That's silly. I wish mom would have told me herself."

"She didn't want to disappoint you."

"It's somewhat of a relief. To be honest, I really don't know Michael. We hadn't seen each other or spoken in years. Not since your wedding. So now I don't have to worry about it. I didn't know what to say anyway. Stephan has to worry about it now."

"But Stephan doesn't know Michael either. He probably has only seen Michael once or twice in his life, if that. You should call mom and talk to her."

Daniel knew that his cousin, Stephan, rarely saw or spoke to Michael but he did not want to agree with Maria. That would mean that he would have to do the eulogy himself.

"There's no point. Once mom makes up her mind, she won't listen to anyone. Besides, I'm sure mom wants a Christian eulogy and Stephan can do that."

Daniel was aware that his mother and his sisters never considered him a true Christian because Daniel stopped going to church years ago after his divorce. It was not unlike his mother to favor someone that she regarded as a real Christian even if they were strangers over non-Christian family members.

"Doesn't Stephan live in Philadelphia?" Daniel asked.

"He does. He flew in yesterday. I heard that he writes off his expenses for tax purposes. This way he can see his family too. That's not right."

Daniel did not want to involve himself anymore in this issue. He knew it would go nowhere and he was relieved that he did not have to spend any more time fretting over the eulogy.

"I haven't seen cousin Stephan in almost twenty years. It will be nice to see him," added Daniel.

"That's not all." Daniel loathed to hear what Maria would say next. "Mom wants you to read the obituary at the funeral."

"Whose bright idea was that? I've never heard of anyone reading an obituary at a funeral before. Have you?"

"I haven't either, but Aunt Isabel says it's done and Cynthia convinced mom that it's done at funerals too."

"It seems like that's just mom's way to include me and not offend me because she asked Stephan to do the eulogy. Can you just tell her that I'm ok with it and I don't need to be involved or read the eulogy?"

"You don't have to write the obituary. Aunt Isabel and Cynthia wrote it already. Cynthia is going to email you a copy so that you can practice it a couple of times before the funeral this afternoon."

Daniel knew that there was nothing that he could do and he did not want to offend his mother at this time so he relented.

"I told Isabel and Cynthia not to mention Michael's suicide attempt in the obituary. Mom believes it's a sin and I don't want her aggravated by that." Maria's voice conveyed concern for her mother that had not been displayed since Lucia moved to Georgia.

"I wouldn't read that even if it was in the obituary. I would skip it," Daniel said confidently.

"Tell me what it says. I don't want Isabel and Cynthia making Michael out to be the greatest son or brother. He wasn't. I'm sorry to say that. But that's the truth. You know how he was. I don't mind that they say nice things about him. Just don't make him out to be a saint." Maria was somewhat anxious and exasperated.

"Uhuh," Daniel responded.

"Just yesterday, Sylvia posted a comment on Facebook that Michael was the greatest brother." Maria proceeded to read it to Daniel. "This is just lies. Sylvia is saying that because she wants to look good to her Facebook friends and garner sympathy from them. She wants mom to think that she had a great relationship with Michael. But Sylvia did not bother with Michael even though she lived across the street. It was all about Sylvia and her kids and that loser husband of hers. I told Sylvia to take the post down, but she refused. I told her that she isn't supposed to lie like that and that she claims to be a Christian..."

At that point, Daniel tuned out. It would not matter what he said to his older sister. Like their mother, Maria would not listen anyway. He waited until she paused. "I think I saw that post. It's still there."

"Yes, it is." Maria was even more infuriated because one could sense that she was trying to subdue her anger. "I'm sure you saw Theresa's post."

"No, I didn't." Daniel wondered what was next.

"Well, Theresa went to the wake on Wednesday evening."

"I was there too, but I didn't see Theresa. I left around five p.m. I couldn't take it after a while to be honest."

"Theresa posted a picture of herself standing over Michael's casket. She was smiling and Roberta was with her. I was so disgusted. It's not appropriate. You could see the bandana over Michael's neck in the picture. I don't know what has gotten over them. No one complained about it either. Cynthia liked the post and so did Lisa. I messaged Theresa right away and told her to take it down. It's a private affair for the family. But nobody stuck up for me. I can't believe it."

Daniel recalled seeing the picture himself earlier that morning, but did not mention it to Maria because that would make matters worse. He had also not said anything to Theresa to take it down even though he felt the picture was morbid and offensive. "Let me check." Daniel opened his Facebook app on his phone and looked for the picture. "It's no longer there."

"I know. After Theresa didn't take the picture down, I called mom about it. She was furious. She almost fainted. She called Theresa immediately and told her to take it down and that it was not Christian of her to do that. Theresa had no right to do that. It's not her son. It's mom's son. So she took it down. But then Cynthia posted that people are high and mighty and think that they are a better Christians than others. I know she was talking about me. But I don't care. It's not right. I know Cynthia is going to come to the defense of her sister, but it's not right. Cynthia should know it too. She claims that she is a Christian too, but I don't see it."

Daniel had seen that post as well: "I don't know what to say. I'm glad that it's down." Daniel just hoped that Maria would not bring up why he never said anything about either posts.

"Anyway, Eduardo just woke up. I'll see you at the funeral. I'm driving mom there." Maria quickly hung up the phone and greeted her husband.

Daniel got dressed in his suit and drove to the funeral home along with Randy. He sat in the front row next to his mother, Lucia, who sat in the aisle seat on the left side of the room. Next to him were Maria and her husband. The rest of the family, Aunt Isabel and Aunt Belén along with their sons and daughters and their children, filled almost half of the small room where the service was held at the Eternal Valley Memorial Park. Some of Michael's friends from elementary school where there. They had read his obituary in the newspaper and were saddened to learn of his passing so young. Members of Lucia's church in Canyon Country also attended. Missing was Jose Luis. Daniel looked for him, but wondered if he would show. He did not bother to call Jose Luis or ask him if he needed a ride. He tried to figure out how Jose Luis would get to the funeral which was nearly an hour away from the motel. After a while, he realized that Jose Luis was not coming so he stopped looking around for him and waited for the service to start.

"Ladies and Gentlemen," Stephan rose to the front and started the service with a short prayer. His daughter, Leticia, stood next to him, assisting in the service. She was also an ordained minister at her church in Temecula. After the prayer, Stephan continued. "I want to introduce the Mendoza family. Lucia Mendoza, please stand up. She is Michael's mother. His siblings, Maria and Daniel, are here as well. Unfortunately, Sylvia and her kids could not make it, but they send their blessings from Georgia." Stephan forgot to mention Jose Luis and then did so once Lucia mentioned her oldest son.

"We are here to celebrate the life of Michael Sheffield. We remember Michael and how his mother had him so late in life. We remember the curly hair he had since he was so young. His bright smile. His willingness to help his mom around the house and go with her to church on Sundays. We remember the times when he would sit quietly in the corner during family get-togethers and when he and his other cousins, Marcus and Raymond and even my daughter, Leticia, would go to Sunday school together when Lucia would visit on the weekends. Now, Michael was not perfect. We all know that. But he had his good parts and we want to focus on that today. Where is he now? Is he in heaven or hell? I don't know. Only God knows. We don't know the decision that he made and whether he gave his life to the Lord. He could have. And if he did, then he is present with the Lord right now. One day, we will meet him with the Lord if that is the decision that he made. I hope to see him there when I go. And I encourage you all to think of what will happen to you when you pass. As the scriptures say: 'Yet you do not know what your life will be like tomorrow. You are just a vapor that appears for a little while and then vanishes away.' Where will you go? Will you be with Michael in heaven? I hope so. Let's pray."

As everyone bowed their heads, Daniel turned and could head Jose Luis walk up the aisle and sit down next to Cynthia and Theresa and their kids. Jose Luis looked over at Daniel as he sat down to talk to his cousins. He was wearing the purple suit and white gloves. Stephan and Leticia lead everyone in a few hymns and then were about to dismiss the service when the funeral director reminded everyone that Michael would be interned immediately. The family exited the building and walked the short distance to the plot near the northern end of the cemetery. Now that Jose Luis had arrived, Lucia asked if he would be a pall bearer and carry the casket from the hearse to the plot. He readily agreed.

After Michael was interned, Lucia said, "This is a lovely view. Michael has a nice spot at the top of the hill and can see the whole valley below. I would like to be buried next to him." She began to sob and Isabel, Maria, and Belén comforted her.

Stephan announced that the reception would be at Jack's house, Lucia's second husband. He passed out directions and told everyone that food was catered and that there were no worries about bringing food for buffet. Jack had paid for everything because he was still in love with Lucia after all those years.

The entire entourage drove the mile and a half to Jack's house. He no longer owned horses like he did when he was younger. He also got rid of the ATVs that the kids used to ride. The family, including Aunt Isabel and cousin Cynthia, began reminiscing about the many times they spent rising horses and playing in the dirt roads near the acreage by Jack's house.

Having lived in Arizona for nearly fifteen years, Daniel was now able to see his cousins and seconds cousins and theirs sons and daughters. He had not seen most of them in decades. Some of them, he never meet before. The joy and camaraderie was pleasant and surprising. The oldest cousin, Lorenzo, announced that Aunt Isabel's family was having a reunion the following summer and invited everyone to come. Daniel vowed that he would attend.

Dear reader,

We hope you enjoyed reading *From The Streets Of Chambers Lane*. Please take a moment to leave a review, even if it's a short one. Your opinion is important to us.

Discover more books by Daniel Maldonado at
https://www.nextchapter.pub/authors/daniel-maldonado

Want to know when one of our books is free or discounted? Join the newsletter at
http://eepurl.com/bqqB3H

Best regards,
Daniel Maldonado and the Next Chapter Team

The story continues in:

When Dreams Abound: A Return To Chambers Lane

To read the first chapter for free, please head to:
https://www.nextchapter.pub/books/when-dreams-abound

About the Author

Mr. Maldonado is an attorney in the Phoenix area that has practiced insurance coverage and employment discrimination law. He is a co-author/editor of Couch on Insurance, a multi-volume treatise on insurance law. Mr. Maldonado is also a contributing author on CAT Claims: Insurance Coverage for Natural and Man-Made Disasters. Mr. Maldonado also wrote the employment chapter for the Arizona Tort Law Handbook. He has contributed to various law reviews and other articles. Now, Mr. Maldonado takes his hand to an area of personal satisfaction: relationships and emotional experiences.

Bibliography

This is a list of books and short stories written and published by Daniel Maldonado:

The Palace of Winds and Other Short Stories - A collection of poignant short stories addressing romance, failures, intrigues, and beliefs from a male perspective.

Through Thunder and Light - A follow up to the original compilation "The Palace of Winds and Other Short Stories."

From the Streets of Chambers Lane - The intriguing story of the Mendoza family's unexpected loss of their youngest son and sibling, Michael. Dealing with spiritual struggles and disillusionment as well as familial rivalries and quirky social interactions, the novella introduces the reader to each diverse family member's perspective of the tragic event while personalizing their cultural past and fears of the unknown future.

When Dreams Abound: A Return to Chambers Lane - Fatherless, Daniel Mendoza learns from a myriad of male friends and neighbors who come into his life from childhood to adulthood about what it actually means to be a man.

The Prodigal Son From Chambers Lane - The oldest son, Jose Luis Mendoza, Junior, battles a haunting past secret that has hindered his growth even into his adult years. He must confront his unloving and hard-hearted mother and others who have betrayed his desire to be loved before he is able to escape it and embrace his future.

From The Streets of Chambers Lane
ISBN: 978-4-82411-036-7 (Mass Market)

Published by
Next Chapter
1-60-20 Minami-Otsuka
170-0005 Toshima-Ku, Tokyo
+818035793528
8th November 2021

www.ingramcontent.com/pod-product-compliance
Lightning Source LLC
LaVergne TN
LVHW032009070526
838202LV00059B/6368